The Ghost Line

THE
GHOST
LINE

ANDREW NEIL GRAY
AND J. S. HERBISON

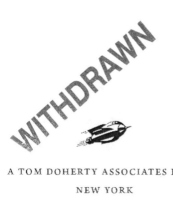

A TOM DOHERTY ASSOCIATES BOOK

NEW YORK

This is a work of fiction. All of the characters, organizations, and events portrayed in this novella are either products of the authors' imaginations or are used fictitiously.

THE GHOST LINE

Cover illustration by John Harris
Cover design by Christine Foltzer

Edited by Carl Engle-Laird

A Tor.com Book
Published by Tom Doherty Associates
175 Fifth Avenue
New York, NY 10010

www.tor.com

Tor® is a registered trademark of
Macmillan Publishing Group, LLC.

ISBN 978-0-7653-9496-5 (ebook)
ISBN 978-0-7653-9497-2 (trade paperback)

First Edition: July 2017

For R and L

Acknowledgments

We'd like to thank Susan Juby and Alan Gray for reading early versions of the manuscript. We'd also like to thank Carl Engle-Laird for having faith in it and for his sharp editorial eye. And finally, thanks to our children for putting up with many, many discussions of plot points and characters during car trips, dinners, walks in the woods, etc.

From fifty kilometers out they could finally see the ship they were going to break into. The *Martian Queen* gleamed in the sunlight, a brilliant white fleck in the darkness between Earth and Mars.

"This better be worth it," Michel said.

"It will be." Saga called up a magnified view on the big screen on the *Sigurd*'s bridge. Even if her husband wasn't excited, she felt the familiar buzz of anticipation. It wasn't just the thrill of a new target. The liner before them was intact and untouched. Not holed, half-melted, or long since abandoned and stripped bare. This job felt like a luxury. Which was fitting, given the ship's history.

Everything about the *Martian Queen* was ostentatious, from her hull paint to the rows of windows that stitched her sides. If her designers could have found an excuse for funnels, propellers, and an anchor, no doubt they would have welded them on.

"Form should follow function," she said. "No wonder they went bankrupt."

"Ha!" Gregor, the *Sigurd*'s pilot, had lived in the aster-oid belt for twenty-five years, but his Russian accent was as thick as the day he left Novosibirsk. He rubbed the stubble on his chin. "You think it was just a way to get from one planet to other? Main function of this liner was to separate people from money."

"Point taken."

An old brochure glowed in Gregor's hands. "Two casinos. Two! Plus steam room and spa. Stage shows. Recreation ring. Even had Michelin-star chef."

Saga saw a line of dancing girls kicking up their heels. The narrator's voice issued from the brochure, followed by tinny orchestral music. She reached over and folded the bright rectangle, turning it off.

"Hey," Michel said. "I was enjoying that."

Saga snorted. "They're probably not even real. Who can kick that high?"

Gregor winked at Michel. "That is good thing. If dancers were synths then maybe they are still in storage. We could have party."

"No parties." Wei floated into the room. The woman who'd hired them wasn't much for entertainment, let alone slacking off. Wei was in her forties, her black hair cut in a belter bob, the short haircut favored by people who spent a lot of time in pressure suits. She wore simple grey coveralls and the strained expression of someone who had reached the limits of her patience. "You have to get inside to have a party."

"Problem?" Gregor said.

"Yeah, this is a worthless piece of shit." Wei threw a small object at Gregor. Surprised, he watched as it pinged off his shoulder.

Michel plucked it out of the air. He looked at the data stick that contained Wei's intrusion package. "We knew this was a possibility, right?"

"And we *did* warn you," Saga added. When they'd first met her, Wei revealed she had the chance to buy a software back door into an unnamed mothballed ship, untouched for twenty years. They'd told her not to waste her money. Saga had sung her and Michel's praises, their ability to insinuate their way into the toughest systems.

But Wei had gone ahead and purchased the package anyway. She shot them a sour look, then pushed off and was gone, back to her room.

Saga looked at her husband. She grinned. "Care to do some hacking?"

"Thought you'd never ask."

～

The *Sigurd* slid under the belly of the *Martian Queen*. Up close, the sheer size of it was apparent. Their sleek cutter was like a lifeboat in comparison.

"Less than one hour," Gregor said. "How did you do it?"

"Just fly the damn ship," Wei snapped.

"Ship knows how to dock herself." Gregor turned to Michel. "I would like to know how you got in. I have all ears."

"We buy old data," Michel said.

"From auctions," Saga continued. "Bankrupt companies sell off assets to pay back creditors, right? Everybody wants marketing information and mineral surveys. Nobody cares about the maintenance logs and system manuals. We get them for almost nothing."

"Ah," Gregor said. "So you have your *own* back doors."

The *Sigurd* slowed as it reached the stern of the *Martian Queen,* aiming for the service docking port near the wedge of reactor shielding.

"We almost never find *actual* programmer back doors," Michel said. "Mostly it's just regular holes. We know every system, every subsystem. How often they were updated. The software hasn't been patched for years, so we had our choice of exploits."

"The one we used was a buffer overflow in the LIDAR sensors," Saga said. She looked at the display in her contact lenses, the interface to the liner floating in front of her face. Cracking the ship's software had been foreplay, a thrill that promised greater rewards to come. When she'd been back on Earth, it had been fooling alarm systems and picking locks. Either way, the goal was the same: breaking in. Turning an abandoned place into a playground.

The *Sigurd* slid closer, cautiously. A meter from contact the service port extended its clamps in welcome. A moment later, with a clunk heard through the ship's hull, they were docked.

"No need to explain more," Gregor said. "I would not understand anyway." He turned to Wei. "You have your ship now."

~

It was almost a day until they left the *Sigurd*. After all her hurry to get there, Wei seemed reluctant to take the next step. She ordered Saga and Michel to remotely explore the security systems inside the *Queen,* to make sure there were no hidden alarms. Then she spent several hours in her cabin, uncommunicative. When she finally emerged, Saga and Michel pushed, but she wouldn't budge. "You two have been exploring for years," she said. "You should know better."

"But you haven't even cleared our survey bots," Saga said. "The *Queen*'s systems all say it has full pressure. We've told it to raise ambient to room temperature."

"We're ready when I say we're ready," Wei growled.

So they sat in the galley. Gregor came by once for a

bulb of tea, which he slurped noisily, but otherwise they were alone.

"You could get started from here," Michel said. "With the *Queen's* internal cameras. You could put together a rough model in half an hour."

Saga shook her head. Long blond tendrils floated in front of her eyes with the movement. She'd taken a shower and washed her hair while they waited. "The resolution would be too low. And you know I need to see a place with my own eyes first. We spent two months getting here, we can wait a little longer."

Michel slapped the table in frustration. "Goddamn it; waiting is all we ever do." The motion pushed his slim body up and he floated toward the ceiling. He waved his arms, reaching for a handhold as Saga laughed. He shot her a look and pushed himself out of the galley.

She gathered her damp hair, fixing it into a bun at the nape of her neck with an elastic from her wrist. He'd be back eventually, apologetic. Of the two of them, he'd always had the shorter fuse, but his anger burned itself out quickly.

In the meantime, she would check her mail, which should have loaded by now. Since this was a dark mission, she'd had to route her request through several anonymous relays scattered around the asteroid belt. What should have been a twenty-minute operation had stretched to three hours.

There was the usual clutter: Comments and suggestions from people who subscribed to her interactives, which she let her concierge software answer. Some sponsorship updates. A few trip proposals from the daredevils and interactive artists who, like Michel and herself, explored the derelict stations, ships, and asteroid habitats that littered the solar system. A request for a private guided tour of a famous wreck from someone who was almost certainly bored and wealthy, looking for an unusual amusement.

And, finally, a note from her aunt.

That one she avoided for a while. She made more tea. The galley could print butter biscuits she particularly liked, and she ate two as she contemplated the liquid in her squeeze cup.

She sighed and opened the message. Aunt Yrsa always began with inconsequentials: they'd had a month of *gluggaveður*—window-weather—in Reykjavík. As if being stuck inside mattered to someone like her; she hadn't lived in a place with a climate for nearly ten years. That was followed by news of the extended family, their various adventures and domestic dramas. Finally, Yrsa got to Saga's mother, Hanna, and the new therapy Saga was paying for. The treatments had already regrown connections and brain tissue, untangled some of the muddle that was her mind. But they'd completed only the first stage, and modern medicine still had its limits.

"She was asking for you," her aunt said. "She thought you were in the next room. Hanna didn't understand she was in a care facility. She kept saying someone had stolen her curtains."

Saga winced and rubbed her temples. She closed the message window, blinked away the interface. There were many things she would prefer to do than think about her mother, a hundred and fifty million kilometers away, believing her only daughter had just stepped out for a moment.

~

At first, Wei had sounded like just another rich tourist. She'd proposed a visit to an unnamed abandoned ship. Michel had replied to her message, telling her sorry, but they were taking a break.

But Wei had been insistent, offering a generous fee. When that didn't work, she'd visited them in person, showing up at the site they were exploring—a failed attempt to hollow out an asteroid habitat. When her ship appeared on their navigation displays, they'd been stunned: nobody met face-to-face in the belt if they had other options. But here Wei was, in the flesh. After a brief exchange, she'd invited them on board the *Four of a Kind*, the ship she was going to use for the expedition.

Michel gave a low whistle when they entered. The ship was an order of magnitude better than anything they'd used before. Faster, larger, much more comfortable.

"This is seriously yours?" he asked.

"My employers provided it," Wei said. They were sitting in the ship's galley, drinking very passable espresso. "They have considerable resources. They'll even pay for a professional pilot. So I need to know: Will you accept the job?"

Saga shook her head. "We already told you we're taking a break."

"This ship's fast. We can be in and out in under four months. Then you can have your vacation." Wei mentioned a higher fee, a bonus structure.

"Starting a family is not a vacation," Michel said.

"Hold on." Saga took her husband aside. "The money's good. Better than good."

"So? We're doing okay."

"I'm not just thinking about us. What about my mother? This could really help her." She hesitated for a moment. "We could even afford to thaw *two*. Maybe spend some time raising them on Earth with their grandmother."

They had stored a dozen frozen embryos in a radiation-protected vault deep inside Ceres—a belter wedding tradition. Once they'd done it she'd put them out of her mind. Insurance against a future she wasn't ready to think about. But Michel came from a large family of French-Guianese Catholics. Every time they went back to Vesta he mooned over his nieces and nephews, dropped unsubtle hints. He had finally convinced her.

She felt a pulse of guilt at the sudden brightening in his eyes.

"Maybe," Michel said after a moment. "But we can't agree to this unless we know all the details first."

They went back to Wei. "Who pays what you're paying just to wander around on an abandoned ship?" Michel asked.

Wei glanced around the small room as if someone could be listening in. "I do," she said. "There's a nondisclosure agreement for you to sign, and then I'll tell you all of it."

"One last request," Saga said. "If we take the job, I want you to change the name of this ship. *Four of a Kind* is . . . Well, she deserves something more adventurous. We all do."

~

When they left the *Sigurd,* they went in pressure suits, Wei in front, followed by Michel and Saga. Gregor, who'd been off duty since they docked, was still in his cabin; he hadn't bothered to come out while they organized to leave. It was an open secret that when he wasn't working, Gregor had a taste for the vodka he'd hacked the ship's bioreactor to brew. He'd always flown sober, so nobody pushed him on it.

They passed through the air lock and bumped into Wei, who'd stopped abruptly. She appeared to be scrutinizing the *Queen's* service bay, a midsize room. It was empty, spotless. After a long moment, Wei pushed herself forward and pulled open one of the cases she was carrying. Saga recognized a high-end chemical sampler.

"It's all green in here, Wei," Michel said. "Do you really need that?"

Saga blinked her suit's environmental interface into life. The readout showed a normal nitrogen-oxygen mix at Earth-standard pressure. A little chilly at fifteen degrees Celsius, but warming up.

"There's still the possibility of contamination," Wei said, not looking up.

"From what?" Michel said. "The Brie going off twenty years ago? The *Queen* was mothballed, right? I don't see anything odd on the suit sensors." He looked around. "No mold on the walls."

Wei didn't respond. She'd been crystal clear in her briefing before they came through the lock: suits on at all times, no matter what. She strapped the sampler to her chest and folded the box away. She pushed against the wall and floated down the service corridor without looking back.

Saga shared a glance with Michel as they followed her, each carrying an equipment case. *Our boss is an odd duck,* he sent in a private message.

She caught his eye, winked, and got a grin in return.

The service corridors were utilitarian, doorways marked in standard ship-script, the letters followed by machine-readable codes for the robots that would have loaded and unloaded supplies and equipment. Wei led them through the warren without hesitation. They had to scramble to keep up, pushing off from walls and handholds, using quick bursts from their suit jets when necessary.

Finally, Wei paused at a set of doors, tapping at the control panel beside them.

"First thing we do," Michel said, breathing heavily, "is we get the gravity back on. Wei, can we at least take our helmets off?"

Wei turned toward them. Her face wasn't visible. She had blanked her helmet's faceplate completely. It gave Saga a momentary shiver, a reminder of those old stories of empty suits prowling abandoned ships.

"I told you, no," Wei said. "The air checks out down here, but we still have the passenger areas to test. That's where contamination is the most likely."

No it isn't. Michel's private message appeared in Saga's field of view. *We all know aft is where anything dangerous would have been kept.*

Just indulge her, okay? She's paying the bills.

They entered the passenger section of the liner, and everything changed.

Unlike the service areas, which were designed for zero gravity, the passenger section was clearly meant to be used under spin. Carpeting on the floors, recessed lights in the ceilings. Wood panels with intricately patterned inlays on the walls. Saga couldn't help but feel disappointed. Decaying structures and damaged ships had so much more character. On previous expeditions she'd imagined ghosts lurking around dark corners, connected with haunting memories of economic collapse or terrible accidents. But here? They could have been in a fancy hotel back on Earth. It didn't even *look* abandoned. The lights were still on.

She kept her thoughts to herself as they passed down three wide corridors, then found themselves at a plainlooking door marked *Crew Only.*

"What's this?"

"Bridge access," Wei said. "You didn't think it would be up front, did you?"

Saga caught Michel's disgusted look. As if they would make such a rookie mistake. Assuming that a luxury liner was essentially a cruise ship with a rocket engine attached to its stern was something Earth tourists would do. As with all spacecraft, the bridge was buried in the middle of the ship, the safest location. She knew from their research that the bow had an observation bubble, but it was covered with shielding to protect against dust grains and micrometeorites.

They floated upstairs to the ship's inner level, through a set of security doors that Michel bypassed with a couple of minutes of work. Then they were inside the bridge: a plainly decorated room with two sets of consoles and a group of chairs fixed to tracks on the floor.

"Okay," Wei said. "Time to earn your keep."

"You're not sticking around?" Michel asked.

"I have things to do." Without another word she turned and jetted away, her suit light flickering as she descended out of sight.

Michel set up their gear. *Here we are,* he messaged. *Alone at last . . .*

Saga smiled. They might have a paranoid and peculiar employer, not to mention a semi-alcoholic pilot. But when it came down to it, at least they still had each other.

~

Even with the ship's manuals and logs, which they'd spent weeks reviewing during the trip to the *Queen*, it still took almost half a day to bring basic systems back online. She'd been mothballed properly, everything kept nice and cool in a low-humidity, low-oxygen environment. Reactor barely burbling along. A few systems reported minor faults, and some cameras and sensors were unresponsive, but the vast majority of the complex and interdependent ecosystem that kept an interplanetary passenger ship humming along was still functional.

Finally, Saga started up the spin mechanisms that provided artificial gravity for the passenger sections. Weight returned slowly, the guest suites settling at a hair above Mars-normal gravity, while the bridge, closer to the liner's center, was less than half that. Saga finished double-checking that the spin systems were all healthy, then looked over at Michel.

"What the hell?" she said. "Why did you take your helmet off?"

He grinned and ran his hand through his close-cropped curls. "I'm not an idiot. I checked all the environment logs first: everything's fine." He made a show of sniffing the air. "It's better than fine. Definitely a step up from my suit."

"Should we be so quick to trust the life support? It's been off for twenty years."

Michel shrugged. "I trust it."

Wei had explained the situation that evening back on her ship after they'd signed her NDA. The *Martian Queen* wasn't a derelict—she was a ghost liner. The company that built and operated her went bankrupt when Earth-Mars traffic collapsed a quarter century ago. The new owners bought her cheap and kept her running so they could hold their claim on passenger services on the orbit, waiting until the economy improved. The law was that as long as the company had a ship making regular runs between Earth and Mars—even if it carried no passengers or crew—they had control of one of the most efficient routes between the two planets. Apparently there were still ghost trains in Europe that did the same thing, traveling empty from city to city.

"That's not what you told us earlier," Saga had said, watching the espresso slosh around in her zero-gee cup. "You said it was abandoned."

"It *is* abandoned." Wei slapped the console in front of her. "Nobody has used it for twenty years. Nor do they plan to. But I'm sure you've seen the news: things are looking up on Mars. There's a market in taking people there."

"But not rich tourists." Michel peered at her, a look

of comprehension on his face.

"Correct. The people I work for want to send colonists. Lots of them. Minimum cost. They're going to hibernate most of the way; nobody needs a casino and a spa."

"They can't just buy the *Queen*?" Michel asked.

Wei shook her head. "It's cheaper to make a new ship than refit one that was never designed for hundreds of hibernation beds. My employers' ships will go slow: no need to rush if everyone's asleep, right?"

Saga got it before Michel did. "You want us to do something to the *Queen*, don't you."

They were to hack the ship. Tweak her course at apoapsis to continue on past Mars into a different orbit, leaving the route open for another company to claim. They'd be doing many honest, hardworking people a favor. They had a responsibility. And Saga could create one of her famous interactives at the same time, though she wouldn't be able to release it until the statute of limitations had passed on their little adventure.

Now they were here, at the helm of the old liner. Saga surveyed the *Martian Queen*'s control systems. Layers of interface floated in her contact lenses, rendered in colors that mapped their functions. Michel was right: environmental control and life support were running flawlessly—the ship had a perfectly safe atmosphere.

"I don't know," she said. "I guess I'm just so used to things being ruined. It's weird to have it all working."

"Not *all* working." Michel gestured at the display in front of him. "We only have low-level control. We still have to break into the nav system without waking up the ship's mind."

That was going to take time. Saga sighed and started opening display windows.

Michel looked at her with a small smile. "You should go," he said. He gestured to her expedition case. "Explore the ship."

"Don't you need me here?"

"We have time. Take a couple of hours; when you're back you can help out."

Saga touched the case, hesitated.

"Go!" Michel said.

~

The cameras buzzed through the air like a swarm of bees. A quick gesture and the eight little spheres spread out in a cloud in front of Saga; then she pulled them back until they circled her head like a halo. Another gesture and they flew in a line back into the case.

Tempting as it was to record everything right away, she was going to explore without video for now. It always took a while to absorb the feeling of being somewhere that had been empty for years, decades. The echoing spaces of mines, bulk haulers, holed habitats. Dioramas of human existence, frozen in time. Eventually, they would speak to her, these places. They would speak and she would begin to create the narratives her fans paid for.

She placed the exploration case on the floor of the corridor and blinked its interface to life, then stood back as the mapping bots emerged. They bumbled and bounced in the low gravity, heading off in all directions to create the submillimeter-scale rendition of the ship she'd use to house her narratives.

"Mapping's on," she said over her suit radio. "Open all the doors for them, will you, Michel?"

She watched as a group of the bots rolled up to the carved wooden doors that led to the ship's bow. The doors opened silently and the bots passed through.

Instead of following them, she went aft, to where the passenger area of the ship began. They'd come in through the service entrance, like servants or coal deliveries in the old days of country houses. The main entrance was where the quality would have boarded the *Queen*.

Finally, a place that wasn't bland and forgettable. Even on a luxury liner, space was at a premium, but the designers had done wonders with what they had. Marble tiles on the floor. Real wood in sweeping curves. An actual crystal chandelier, hung with glittering stars around blue-white and red blown-glass orbs at the center, symbolizing the two planets the ship connected.

She imagined the entrance in her narrative. A user would wander the dark and empty corridors, then suddenly find themselves back in the ship's heyday. The laughter and chatter, the clink of champagne glasses. Passengers and crew channeling the luxury liners of old. Rockefellers and Astors and oysters on the half shell. Something unusual would happen then; she didn't know what yet, but it would come to her.

As she turned, wondering if the chandelier would need enhancement, she caught movement in her peripheral vision. She peered down one of the corridors that led from the entrance area. It felt as if someone had just been there. It felt like she had been observed.

She called over the open channel. "Wei?"

Wei's voice crackled in her ears. "Problems?"

"That wasn't you, was it?"

"What wasn't me?"

"Are you at all near the entranceway?"

"I'm back on the *Four*—I mean the *Sigurd*," Wei said. "Aren't you and Michel supposed to be hacking the navigation system right now?"

Saga turned up the magnification and light amplification on her suit visor. No one was there. "Michel has it under control. I'm just getting my bearings for the inter-active."

"You're counting chickens is what you're doing." Wei sounded sour. "When you should be sitting on eggs. You can play *after* you hack my ship. Is that clear?"

"Crystalline," Saga said. She imagined Michel back in the control room, perched on an ostrich egg, and snorted.

There was a moment of silence on the line, then a click as Wei disconnected.

"Oops."

She examined the corridor before heading back. It was empty, but again she felt as if her presence had inter-rupted something. She had wandered onto a stage being set for a play. Around her there were nooks in the walls for vases of flowers, art panels to display paintings. If she concentrated, she could almost hear the fading echo of a violin. On the maiden voyage there had been a string quartet to greet passengers. How much money would it have cost to send four musicians to Mars and back, just to provide pleasant background noise?

She came to a set of doors. More carved wood. Luxury hiding the necessity of pressure doors. She touched them, but they remained closed.

Saga traced the carving, a bas-relief of battling galleons, clouds of smoke rising from the cannons in their sides. Then she saw something strange: a twig protruded from the wood, its bark a dark grey. A tiny brown oak leaf dangled, no bigger than her thumb.

She touched the twig and it bent under her gloved finger, the sensors in her suit conveying its pliant feel. When she stroked the leaf, it broke off and spiraled slowly to the floor. "Shit," she muttered. If there was anything she hated, it was thoughtless vandalism. Finding a derelict site with graffiti sprayed across surfaces, objects destroyed for no good reason. It always made her furious. And now she'd damaged something on the *Queen*.

She picked up the leaf to inspect it, using the magnifier in her faceplate. As far as she could tell, it was an actual leaf. An autumn leaf, growing from a real twig.

～

"Of course it's not a real leaf," Michel said, barely looking up from his programming. "One of the carvers probably glued it on. Like an Easter egg in an interactive."

"But how could it have lasted so long?" she said. "The *Queen* was in service for almost thirty years before it was mothballed."

"Then the mothball team did it as some sort of joke. You can't imagine it grew there, on a dead piece of oak."

"It isn't just the leaf; I thought I saw something moving. Like I was being watched."

"You always do, though, don't you?" Michel had a familiar, faraway look. His attention was captured by his work.

Saga bristled. "This was different. It *felt* different."

"Mmm-hmm."

Saga glared at her husband, but he didn't notice that, either. She slipped the leaf into her pocket. It wasn't worth talking to him about the uncanny; she didn't know why she kept it up. To him, if it couldn't be measured, it didn't exist.

~

Saga and Michel worked until hunger forced them to stop and retreat to the *Sigurd*, where they had a quiet dinner in the galley. Wei had already eaten: the evidence of her half-finished meal lay in the composter. There was no sign of Gregor.

"You didn't make it to the dining room, did you?" Michel was eating a sticky green mixture of algae and seaweed. A few grains of rice floated above his plate, and Saga reached over and plucked them from the air. She mashed them to the side of the container that held her own meal, a rehydrated vegetable stew.

"Just the main entrance hall. Wei ordered me back."

Saga couldn't help rolling her eyes.

Michel grinned at her. "Imagine sitting at a table under gravity. Eating off china plates. You think the galley has any food left in it?"

"If it does, twenty years of storage isn't going to make it taste any better than that muck you're eating."

"Candlesticks," Michel said, waving his fork. "Roasted meat. A butler to buttle whenever you need him. Cigars and brandy."

"And would the ladies all retire to the drawing room after dinner, leaving the gentlemen to talk about politics?"

"Something like that." Another grin. "But since we can't have a formal dinner, I have another idea."

Saga raised an eyebrow, but he wouldn't say any more. "Later," he said. "You'll see."

When they were done, she pinged Wei. Somehow, knocking on the door of her room seemed more intrusive than sending her a message. It took a minute to get a response.

Are you finished? Wei replied.

We're here on the Sigurd. *Come on out.*

It took another few minutes for Wei to emerge, meeting them on the bridge. She looked tired, dark circles under her eyes.

"What's wrong?" Wei asked. "What happened?"

Saga blinked, surprised by the wobble in the other

woman's voice. "Nothing's wrong. We just thought you'd want an update."

Wei looked from her to Michel. "Oh," she said, deflating a little.

Michel started telling her about the ship's systems. How just getting basic access hadn't given them the level of control they needed to change the *Queen*'s course. It was going to take time.

Wei interrupted. "You told me you were good at this."

"We *are* good," Michel said. "We'll get there."

Saga cleared her throat. "Also, I wanted to talk about the money. You said we'd get a milestone payment when we boarded the *Queen*." She paused, looking at Wei. "We're on board, as you'll have noticed."

"It's not like the casino is open," Wei finally said. "Where are you going to spend it?"

"We had a deal." Michel glanced at Saga. "And some of us have bills to pay."

"Fine," Wei said. "You'll get your payment. I'll transfer it now." She turned and pushed out of the room.

Saga sighed. "She's been like this ever since we came near the *Queen*. What the hell's her problem?"

"I don't know," Michel said, "and I don't care." He put their dishes in the cleaner and sealed it tight. Then he held out his hand.

"What?"

"Just trust me. You won't be disappointed."

~

Michel pushed open the doors. "Voilà!"

The presidential suite lay before them. Carpet the color of Mars, a separate bedroom, what looked like authentic antique furniture. Saga crossed to the bathroom.

"God, it even has a bathtub." She stood and stared. Midnight blue with ornate copper fixtures, it was big enough to fit the two of them comfortably.

She turned around. Michel had shed his suit and was lying across the bed in his one-piece undersuit. He patted the covers beside him.

Saga hesitated. She told herself Wei was just being overly cautious. Every atmosphere reading had been nominal since they came aboard. She reached up and cracked her helmet seal. Sniffed cautiously. The room smelled fine.

"Hurry," Michel said. "There's a pressure emergency I need your help with." He glanced down at his groin in mock alarm.

"I'm sure there is," she said. She put her helmet down and slowly unbuckled the suit's torso connectors, wiggling her hips as she did. "Let's see what we can do about that."

Their lovemaking was fast and furious, a release of pent-up tension after two months of awkward and furtive zero-gee coupling. Afterward, they lay tangled in the sheets. She found the lighting controls, and a mock aurora played on the far wall, streams of shimmering colored light.

It reminded her of Iceland. "I have to bring you home to show you the *norðurljós,*" Saga said.

"Hmm?" Michel's eyes were half-closed.

"We could take my mother with us. Go out into the countryside." *If the therapy works.* She left the thought unsaid. Bad luck to speak it. She'd transferred the money as soon as Wei paid them. It would have been enough to buy her mother a new house. It *was* going to work.

"You and your elusive elves." Michel rolled over, pulling the sheets up to his shoulders.

"The Huldufólk are part of our culture, you heathen. Lots of us believe in them." But he was already asleep.

She lay there for a while, listening to his breathing deepen. She turned off the aurora, put the room in sleep mode, let her mind drift.

She jerked awake. It felt like only moments had passed, but she knew she'd probably slept for hours. Her bladder was insistent on this point.

After the luxury of a gently warmed toilet seat, she walked back toward the bed, then veered away, opening the doors of the closet. It was half the size of their cabin on the *Sigurd* and contained a room safe, a clothing cleaner/presser, a pair of silk bathrobes in blue and rose. But also, unexpectedly, several sets of clothes. Formal wear: a tuxedo, a black dress. The fabric felt new under her fingers. The dress even looked to be her size.

Saga smiled. Michel must have ordered it from the ship's printer. He could still surprise her with small acts of thoughtfulness.

In the top drawer of the dresser she found a selection of women's underwear. She put on a black bra and bottoms, then slipped into the dress. She admired herself in a floor-length mirror. "My hair looks like an untrimmed hedge," she muttered. But the dress was lovely.

She didn't feel like sleeping. The ship was out there, unexplored. Her lenses activated, she turned on the map and left the suite. She headed aft, padding down the corridor barefoot. The interior lighting was set to a soft nighttime glow.

Exploring on her own was what she liked best. Not that doing it with Michel wasn't a pleasure. They'd met on a group expedition, a trip to one of the first asteroid mines, now a warren of machine-bored tunnels and cavernous empty spaces. But she couldn't make her art without solitude.

Although Michel now accepted it as part of her character, he didn't understand it. He liked company, the hub-bub of conversation, banter, and joking. In the early days of their relationship, he'd been hurt when she'd gone off by herself for hours. It was all very well to explore in a group, she had tried to explain to him, but any sense of the sacred, of the mysterious, vanished with other people around.

Saga yawned.

The carpeted corridors of the *Martian Queen* were anything but sacred and mysterious. Perhaps this was why she'd imagined she was being watched the day be-fore. Her mind was restless, playing tricks. She focused her attention on details instead. On the nautical history the *Queen* evoked.

She came across a series of display cases, each one housing a model of a famous passenger liner from history. The *Olympic*, the *Queen Mary*. Even the ill-fated *Titanic* had a place of honor, aptly placed near an entrance to the lifeboats.

And then she realized where she was heading. The destination she hadn't consciously selected, but that had been on her mind ever since Michel mentioned it. The main dining room.

~

She hesitated at the doorway; she could see no obvious handle or opening controls. Through her lenses she had access to her suit computer, which in turn connected to the *Queen's* systems. She could probably work out how to get in.

As she considered whether it was worth the effort, there was a click, and the doors swung open. Inside the room, she saw the glint of candlelight. People in formal dress. The murmuring sound of conversations and the clink of silverware. At one corner a man carved slices of roast beef. The scene looked exactly like the picture from Gregor's brochure.

Then the figures flickered and she knew them for what they really were: projections. Still, she walked in cautiously, her heart thudding in her chest. The diners were dressed in clothes whose styles were decades out of date. "Hello?" she said to a woman in a silvery dress who stood at the head of the first table. The woman didn't respond. This wasn't like one of her interactives. It must have been a recording of something that had happened on the ship long ago.

Saga touched a table, expecting her hand to pass through the silverware, but instead felt the cold smoothness of metal. Everything was real. The white linen tablecloth and napkins. The crystal stemware. Stacks of plates on a side table in the *Martian Queen's* own china pattern.

Saga sat down at an empty table set for two. She picked up a silver salt shaker, tipped it cautiously. A sprinkling of grains fell on the table and she touched one with a finger, brought it to her lips. She was mildly surprised to find it was actually salt.

She found a hallmark on the bottom of the salt shaker. It was the real thing. She remembered polishing her grandmother's silver as a girl, admiring the way the dark metal had transformed into something gleaming and beautiful. The salt shaker and the cutlery were untarnished, as if they had just received a good polishing.

A movement drew her gaze; a man was sitting directly across from her. He had very dark skin, several shades darker than Michel's. Unlike the other projections, he wasn't in formal wear; he had on something similar to the undergarments she and Michel wore beneath their pressure suits. The man didn't fit the atmosphere of formality and fun. His face was troubled. She frowned, and he met her eyes. She jumped, dropping the salt shaker.

He was looking through her, of course, not *at* her. Even so she averted her gaze, uncomfortable. When she looked back he was gone. An older man in a mustard-colored turban sat in his place, laughing as he put a forkful of meat into his mouth.

Saga felt a shiver run along her spine.

She needed her cameras. She was going to capture

this. Pin it down. Whatever it was, it would become part of her interactive.

But when she finally returned with her gear the projections were gone, the room silent. She stood in the entrance for a moment, disappointed. Then there was a clattering noise. It sounded again. It was coming from the far side of the room, behind the bar.

She quickly interfaced with the expedition case. A flight of cameras emerged, buzzing. "Go," she whispered.

They sped across the room in formation, a composite picture of what they saw displayed in a window on her lenses. They hovered above the bar, holding position there.

In the video feed, she saw a figure crouched beside a cabinet door. The figure turned and a familiar grizzled face looked up at the cameras with surprise. Then a flash and the feed cut out.

Saga stormed across the room. "What did you do to my cameras?"

Gregor stood up, red-faced. He pointed a finger at her. "You," he spluttered. "You scared living fuck out of me."

He was in his pressure suit, his helmet off. Her camera bugs lay around him on the bar top and the floor.

One of them twitched slightly, a dying insect. She picked it up. It was scorched. Saga brandished it in Gregor's face, furious. "You know how much these cost?"

Gregor had the courtesy to look sheepish. He gestured at his suit. "Is military surplus," he said. "Sometimes I forget it has perimeter defense system. It thought your equipment was attack swarm."

"Then turn the damn thing off. What if it decides *I'm* an attack swarm?"

Gregor muttered to himself, but he tapped at a control pad on his sleeve and assured her the suit was safe. He looked at her then, his gaze traveling from her feet to her face. She glared back at him.

"You brought this dress with you?" he said.

"None of your business. What the hell are you doing in here?"

"Exploring," he said. "Like yourself."

Saga peered at the cabinets behind the bar. She pushed past him and bent over, wishing her dress were less revealing. One of the cabinet handles was battered and scratched. "*Fokking fok,* Gregor. You were trying to break this open," she said. She turned and glared at him. "Why?"

"Perhaps there is treasure inside."

Saga frowned. "You could have asked Michel or me. We have low-level system access, you know."

Gregor shrugged. He looked pointedly at her dress. Her bare feet. "There is more than one way to open door, and you seemed . . . occupied. So you will help me now?"

"Why would I do that?"

Gregor picked up a cutting laser from the toolbox beside him and pointed it at the handle.

Saga looked at the polished wood of the cabinet. The thought of Gregor taking an industrial cutting tool to an antique was abhorrent. "Just hold on a minute. Jesus, Gregor."

She moved back and blinked her lenses to life, quickly flicking through the interface until she found her connection to the *Queen's* OS. It took only a minute to find the dining-room controls. A moment later, the cabinet clicked.

Gregor grunted with pleasure and opened the door. Lined up on the shelves were bottles of spirits, all full.

"*That's* what you were looking for? I thought the *Sigurd* made all you could drink."

Gregor chuckled. "Bioreactor alcohol is a drink only in name. But this. This is real thing." He brought out a triangular amber bottle and cradled it in his arms.

"Won't it be too old?"

Gregor laughed, a deep belly laugh that shook him. "Old is okay. Better than okay. Do you know nothing about good drink?"

She knew more about bad drink than she had ever wanted to know.

"Just . . ." She frowned. "Just don't ruin the place. Put the laser away."

"We are changing ship's orbit, no? Sending it out into the dark. What does it matter what I do?"

"It matters." She was going to say something about beauty. About fragile things and how rare they were. But Gregor's attention was focused on the bottles arrayed in front of him. "Clear out of this room when you're done. Okay?" She picked up her video bugs and deposited their dead forms on a silver tray on the bar top. A burnt offering. At least she had another set on the *Sigurd*.

Gregor watched her, the bottle clutched tight in his hand as if she might snatch it from him. "What were you doing with those?"

"Nothing," Saga said. She turned and walked out. "Nothing at all."

~

After Saga crept back to the suite, she undressed and slid in beside Michel. Sleep was slow to come: she finally drifted off after rehashing her encounter with Gregor a dozen times.

She and Michel made love again in the morning, more slowly this time. Satisfied, they indulged in the luxury of a bath. Then hunger and the knowledge that they had work to do drove them back to the *Sigurd*.

The air lock was sealed. Saga called Wei on the common band. "Open the door, please." There was no answer.

Finally, after her fifth attempt, there was motion on the other side of the lock. Wei came through from the ship. She was wearing her coveralls. "I told you to keep your suits on," she said. "What else did you do? Did you eat anything?"

"Come on, Wei." Saga stuck her helmet up against the glass. "What would we eat? We just spent a night in one of the rooms." She frowned. "How did you know we took our suits off? Have you been spying on us?"

Wei's expression was serious. "I get security alerts. I saw a woman in a dress walking around barefoot in the middle of the night. Why did you meet Gregor in the dining room? What were you plotting?"

Saga glanced at Michel. She hadn't yet told him about her nighttime excursion. "Not plotting," she said. "Exploring. I couldn't sleep. And I didn't even know Gregor was on the *Queen* until I bumped into him." She turned back to the window. "What business is it of yours? Just let us in. We need to eat before we can get back to work."

Wei pushed away and floated back into the *Sigurd*. The ship's inner lock closed behind her, then there was a click. The door before them unsealed with a hiss. Inside the air lock there were three cases, as well as a transparent plastic water canister.

"What's this?" Michel said.

"Breakfast." Wei's face appeared at the *Sigurd*'s window. "And lunch. Dinner. Enough for Gregor, too, since he's joined you in ignoring my rules."

Michel swore. *"C'est quoi ce bordel?"*

Saga understood. "You're not letting us back in, are you."

"I can't," Wei said. "Not yet. I'm still running contamination tests. Until they're complete, I won't take the chance. Go and do your job."

"Contamination with what?" Michel pushed himself over to the *Sigurd* and put his faceplate against the window, glaring at Wei.

"I told you," Wei said. "I told you to keep your suits on."

"And what happens if we finish hacking the ship before you finish your tests?" Saga said.

"I'll know by then," Wei said. "Don't worry."

Michel banged on the window, but Wei was already turning away. She gave them one last disappointed look before disappearing.

Saga grabbed two of the cases and pushed herself back into the *Queen*'s service bay. "Come on," she said.

"She's fucking letting us in," Michel said. He hit the *Sigurd*'s window again, a futile gesture that pushed him backward.

Saga felt a surge of frustration. "You must have learned enough about her by now to know when she's being serious."

Michel turned. "So what? We just go?"

"Yes," Saga said. "We just go." She pulled herself toward the exit. She didn't look back, but she could imagine the look on his face, the last frustrated thump on the lock. The grudging way he would collect the third case and the water canister and follow her.

~

"We should have stayed," Michel said. "Wei would have let us in eventually."

"Just leave it." They'd taken their suits off when they returned to the bridge; no need to pretend any longer. Now they were deep into the systems of the *Queen*. In the center of the room a hologram showed a visual representation of the software that controlled the ship, like a package they'd carefully unwrapped. A grey cloud represented the *Queen's* mind, the weak AI that normally served as an interface to the rest of the systems. They'd walled it off, kept it in the computer equivalent of deep sleep. The *Queen* had been built before the most recent restrictions on AIs, and the possibility of its mind being smart enough to understand what they were up to before they could hack it properly was too great to chance.

As they dug around in the code, Saga could tell Michel was still distracted from the way he kept glancing at her. At last he sighed. "I can't let it go."

"You're going to have to. What good will it do?"

"Why did you let Wei push us around back there?" It came out of him petulantly. "And what the hell was she talking about? You were wandering the ship in a *dress*? Talking to Gregor in the dining room in the middle of the night?"

Saga blinked her displays to sleep. "You printed that dress for me. I put it on when I couldn't sleep." She was still angry at Gregor. "I caught the moron about to use a cutting laser on a bar cabinet, trying to get at the ship's booze."

Michel looked puzzled. "Print for you? What are you talking about?"

"The black dress. It was hanging in the closet of our room, with your tuxedo."

"I didn't have anything to do with that."

Saga frowned. "The *Queen*'s mind's been asleep the whole time. Hasn't it?"

Michel hesitated.

"Hasn't it?"

He looked away. "Well . . . I had to wake up part of it to get housekeeping running."

Saga thought of the dining room, set for dinner and alive with the projected recordings of some antique party. She'd certainly been dressed to join in. "What did you ask it to do?"

Michel looked sheepish. "It might have prepared our room."

She sighed. "You should have talked to me first. You know we can't wake up the ship yet."

"It was just the housekeeping sections. If it was a person, it would be no more than a weird dream."

"But it's *not* a person. Neural networks can connect in all sorts of unexpected ways." She glared at him. "You could have messed everything up—all because you wanted to get laid in a proper bed."

Michel glared back at her, his jaw set. "I didn't, though. Everything's fine." He ran his hand through his hair. "What is it about this gig? Everyone's so bloody tense."

"Maybe it's because some of us actually *want* to be here."

Michel winced. "Not fair."

Silence hung between them.

"Sorry," she said. She wasn't, but she'd been married long enough to know that sometimes you had to say it anyway. Saga got up. "I need a break."

～

She stood outside the dining room doors. Again she found herself at the one place on the *Queen* that felt out of the ordinary. The hall lights were at daylight intensity now, their illumination diminishing the dreamlike quality of the night before. She stepped forward and the doors swung open.

Saga walked into an empty room. The silverware, the plates, all of it gone. Even the tables had vanished. The carpet was impeccably clean. She searched for evidence of the night before, but all she could make out were the faint indentations of table and chair legs.

The silver tray was still on the bar. She picked it up and her damaged camera bugs rattled against each other. "Russian asshole," she muttered. She tossed one of the useless spheres across the room. Halfway through its slow arc it stopped, hovered, then darted back to her, waiting for a command. She felt the breeze from its translucent wings.

"You're supposed to be dead." She blinked her lenses to life. When she connected to the bugs every status indicator said the same thing: they were all active, all reporting full charges and no mechanical problems. The prickle she'd felt the night before returned, followed by a grudging realization: she'd have to show this to Michel.

Back at the bridge, Michel studied one of the bugs.

"I *saw* the scorch marks," Saga said. "They were dead as flies on a windowsill."

He looked skeptical. "Obviously not. Otherwise they'd still be dead. Could they have self-repaired?"

Saga shook her head. "You know better than that. The bugs are too basic to repair themselves. First the leaf, and now this: something strange is happening on this ship."

"*Res ipsa loquitur.*"

Saga blinked. "You speak Latin now?"

"Only when it makes me sound smart," Michel said, a hint of a smile on his lips. "The thing speaks for itself, right? If your drones can't self-repair then they were never broken in the first place. They probably just overheated and shut down, then came back on when they'd cooled."

"Then where'd the scorch marks go?"

Michel turned the silver bug in his hand. It looked as if it had just come out of the fabricator. "Housekeeping cleaned the room, right? It cleaned your bugs, too. I know you love your mysteries, and I'm sure your viewers will eat up all that ghost-ship stuff, but let's face it—the *Martian Queen* is only haunted by us."

Saga snatched the bug from him. "You always have an answer, don't you."

Michel smiled an infuriating smile. "There always *is* an answer."

~

They cracked the nav system soon after dinner. The ship's AI was loosely modeled on a human brain, and the secret lay in fooling the area most comparable to the fusiform gyrus, the part of a human mind that controls recognition: of faces, objects, landmarks. When Wei interfaced with it, the AI would see her as its old captain, resurrected from the *Queen's* memories.

Michel finished his testing and sat back in the chair, a satisfied look on his face. "Do you know if Gregor found any champagne in that bar of his?"

"Cocky," Saga replied. "We still have to actually do it in real life. If we wake the ship up all the way and your hack doesn't work, it's going to put a hard lock on everything. Not to mention screaming alarms back to the company."

"It will work," he said.

"What are you waiting for, then?" Saga said. "Tell Wei the good news."

Wei arrived in her pressure suit fifteen minutes after they contacted her. She listened, her expression hard to read behind her visor, as Michel explained what they'd done. Finally she interrupted him, midsentence.

"Okay," she said. "Stop telling me you can do it and just do it. Wake up the ship."

Michel glanced at Saga and she saw a kernel of doubt.

He'd had it before—the moment of triumph when he cracked a difficult system, followed by the fear that he'd been overconfident. He'd messed it up somehow and it was all going to fail. Of course, it rarely did, but that didn't seem to help. The last of her irritation with him ebbed away when she saw his vulnerability.

"It's a good hack, Michel," she said. "It really is."

They worked together, bringing the mind online the way it would have been woken after an official mothballing. Low-level systems first, then increasingly higher-level processing, each part of the mind performing systemwide self-checks as it activated. The dim holographic map of the mind lit up section by section, like a city recovering from a power failure. When it was complete, Saga held her breath. The hologram flickered, then was replaced by a blinking square that floated in the middle of the room: the ancient symbol of a mind ready for input.

Michel grunted and she realized he'd been holding his breath too. He gestured to Wei. "The *Queen* is yours."

Saga thought she saw an eagerness flash across Wei's face.

"Ship," Wei said. "Open the navigation controls."

"Yes, Captain." The ship's voice was gender-neutral, shading toward female. The navigation interface blossomed within the holographic display in the middle of the room.

"Lock access to me."

"Yes, Captain."

Wei turned to Saga and Michel. "Good work." She paused. "We'll be going in twenty hours, so make sure you clean up your stuff. We don't want to leave any sign we were here."

"What?" Saga stood up, shocked. "You're joking. We spent two months getting here."

"It's not *that* big a ship," Wei said. "How long could it possibly take to do your interactive?"

"I'm not going to rush my recording," Saga said. "You owe us this, Wei."

"I owe you *money*. And you'll get it. But we don't have time to loiter. Once the *Queen's* course changes, someone's going to notice."

While Michel and Wei discussed the navigation interface, Saga brought up her mail queue. A batch had come in while they were busy hacking and she'd ignored it at the time. A red exclamation point flashed in her lenses. Her aunt's name.

She opened the urgent message and felt a drop in her guts, the sensation that gravity had vanished without warning and she was falling and she was going to fall forever.

She must have made a noise, though she had no conscious awareness of it. Both Michel and Wei were looking at her. "What is it?" Michel said.

Saga opened her mouth, but nothing came out. She stared at them dumbly. Finally she forced the words past her lips: "My mother died."

"Oh," Michel said. "Oh, Saga."

He came closer and put his hand on her arm. She shrugged it away, trying to concentrate on the words, reading them again as if somehow they would change. They would admit the message was a mistake. They'd tell her someone else's mother had died.

A cytokine cascade, her aunt wrote. *That's what the doctors told us. Her body rejected the therapy and her immune system went haywire. They tried to save her, but it all happened so quickly . . .*

Michel touched her arm again. "It was my fault," she said. Her throat was tight. The world contracted around her. She clutched at her husband to keep herself upright.

"No," Michel said. He held on to her tightly. "You know that's not true."

"I kept pushing," she said. "I could have left her alone. She was happy enough as she was, but I thought that if we tried the new treatment, something better . . ."

"You wanted your mother back," he said. "That's all. There wasn't anything wrong with that."

"It was for me, it wasn't for her. I was being selfish."

"Shh," Michel said. He stroked her hair. "It's okay."

But it wasn't okay. It wasn't going to be okay. Saga let go of Michel. "I'm going back to the *Sigurd*. I need to call my aunt."

"Ah," Wei said. "About that . . ."

Michel turned and stared at Wei. "You're not serious. You're still quarantining us?"

Wei didn't reply.

"What the fuck is *wrong* with you?" Michel left Saga and wheeled on Wei. He pushed her backward, his face red. "Let my wife back in the ship, now!"

"No," Wei said.

Michel grabbed her upper arms and she reached out and gripped his arms in turn. Frozen, Saga watched the two of them grapple. Michel's eyes widened as Wei forced his arms back, her suit's power assistance giving her the advantage.

"Enough!" Saga yelled, a burning anger in the pit of her stomach. "My mother's dead and you're acting like children."

Wei let go and Michel rubbed his arms, glaring at her furiously. "You can't do this," he said.

"Stop it," Saga snapped. "Both of you." She turned to Wei, who regarded her warily. "I need to talk to my aunt."

"You don't have to be on the *Sigurd*," Wei said. "I can patch the call through your suit. With the relays it'll take thirty minutes or more to get your message to her."

"Not good enough," Michel said.

"It's going to have to be."

Saga suddenly felt tired. "Just connect me, Wei. I need to talk to my aunt more than I need to fight about this."

~

Saga sent her message from the presidential suite, barely keeping her composure as she addressed the camera in her suit's helmet.

"I want to be there," she told her aunt. "I want to touch her before she's gone." Her family were still traditional; there would be a home farewell, with friends and family gathering before they took the white casket to church for the funeral. "But I can't."

They were almost at the *Queen's* maximum distance from Earth. She'd done the math. Even if she stole the *Sigurd*—the wild thought had occurred to her as she walked back to the suite—it still would take more than forty days to get back home.

Her mother would have been six weeks dead by then. The casket long since buried. Saga's absence from the group of mourners, from her family, like the gap of a missing tooth.

She lay on the bed until the reply finally came. The funeral plans were already in motion. Her aunt included a list of the relatives who would be coming from various parts of Iceland and the rest of the world. A cousin was even descending from Luna, at some expense. And Saga's father, Ólafur. He would be there too.

She felt a hot spark of anger at the thought of *him* being there while she was stuck on this ship, cut off from almost everyone she loved.

She got up from the bed. She needed to move.

~

When Saga reached the main entrance hall it seemed smaller and less impressive than the first time she'd been there. The ship was fully awake now; the lights brightened as she moved through the corridors. Doors opened and closed for her. But it felt soulless. Empty.

Her mother's room in the care facility would be empty now too. Sterilized. As if nobody had slept in her bed, brushed her hair in front of the mirror, asked after her absent daughter.

Saga came to the carved doors where she'd found the twig and leaf. She ordered the ship to keep them closed and searched for the twig. Frowned. Searched again. Ran her fingers over the wood, feeling for any strange bumps. But there was nothing.

It was this exact spot: the cannons firing, the cloud of

smoke rising from the side of the battleship. She had a moment of doubt. Was her memory faulty?

Saga dug in her pocket for the leaf but could find only fragments. She sighed and walked through the doors. Signs pointed the way to the ship's spa, the exercise room. She wandered aimlessly, taking turns at random.

After several minutes she passed through another pair of carved doors and entered the casino. Antique gaming machines flickered to life, vying for her attention. Gilt-framed mirrors caught her reflection. To the left of the room, there was a gleaming wood-and-metal bar with racks of empty shelving. Along the back stretched a stage with a purple velvet curtain. There was a round table and two chairs positioned in front. Sitting at one, an empty bottle in front of him, was Gregor. He sat so still she hadn't noticed him at first.

As she approached, he looked up at her. His eyes were tired, dark circles beneath them. "The lovely Saga," he grumbled. "I am in trouble?"

"I don't care what you do on your off time." She took the seat opposite. His pungent sweat had a sour alcoholic note. She nodded at the bottle. "You have any more of that?"

Gregor raised an eyebrow. "You did not drink on trip here."

"Things have happened."

He frowned at her. "Things have *not* happened." He motioned to the stage. "I sit, I wait. Nobody sings to Gregor."

Saga followed his glance. What was the show on the brochure? Dancing girls? It seemed hard to imagine. She looked back at him. "I have no more drink here," he said. "Back in my room there are bottles. Very fine plum brandy . . ."

Saga shook her head. Getting drunk with Gregor suddenly seemed like a bad idea.

"Ship," she called out. "Can you get me a glass of water?"

The ship responded immediately: "Certainly." There was a whirring noise from the bar as a drink dispenser came to life.

Gregor glanced at the bar. "Ship is awake."

"We have full access now. Wei wants to leave tomorrow."

"She tells me go, I go." He stood up, touching the edge of the table to balance himself. He didn't seem as drunk as the empty bottle suggested. "Very well. Since you do not wish plum brandy, I have things to do."

He walked toward the casino's exit, then stopped. Saga watched as he picked up her glass of water from the bar and brought it back to her. He sat down at the table again. "I see it now. Something is wrong."

Saga closed her eyes. "My mother died." It was strange to say the words. They didn't feel true.

"Ah." A silent pause. "It is not such an easy thing, is it? My father passed when I was working in the belt. I could not return for two years. Even if there is . . . complicated relationship, the death of a parent is still important. It has weight."

"It was my fault."

"Then that is even greater burden to carry."

She could feel the weight of that burden. It was a dark, smothering thing. Then Gregor's rough hand on hers. She opened her eyes and jerked her hand back.

"I mean nothing like that," Gregor said. He stood up again. "Come. Please. I have something I would like to show you."

~

They walked in silence. Saga soon realized he was taking her to the recreation ring. It was a part of the ship she hadn't bothered to visit, but she remembered it from their research. A cylindrical room that spanned the entire circumference of the spin section. One of those novelties of habitat and ship design that let you walk in a complete circle, held to the floor by spin, the heads of other people visible above you. Alarming and exotic the first time you did it, a forgettable cliché the tenth time.

"I've been on rings before, you know," Saga said as they came to the entrance.

Gregor smiled. "Humor me."

They entered a dim vestibule. There was a second set of doors ahead, and Gregor motioned to her to continue. She walked out into winter. He joined her as she gaped at the scene. They could almost have been outside on Earth. Snowflakes drifted down from a pale sky above. She could make out the shapes of white hills and trees in the distance. Before them, a glassy surface.

"Here." Gregor handed her a jacket and motioned to a bench by the side of the doors. Several pairs of skates lay there, unlaced.

Saga's breath plumed like smoke.

She turned to Gregor. "How?"

"It is normally pool with small beach." Gregor zipped his own jacket and sat down on the bench. "You could swim laps of ship, see water above, make faces." He pulled an exaggerated expression of surprise and wonder, pointing upward. "Look, it doesn't fall on us!"

Saga glanced at the skates. "You froze the pool."

Gregor smiled. "There is winter setting. You and Michel are not only ones who can make hacks. You and I, we are northern people, no? This is a little like home."

She put on the jacket, slid out of the slippers she'd

been wearing, and pulled on the skates. She waited a moment as they adjusted to her feet, then she laced them, the frigid air beginning to numb her fingertips. In a jacket pocket she found a pair of knit gloves and pulled them on. In the other pocket there was a knit cap.

The cold air prickled her cheeks and numbed the tip of her nose. Iceland was warmer than it used to be, but it still kept the traditions of winter, and sometimes there were cold snaps. Saga had skated on school trips and with friends when she was older. After a few wobbling moments on the ice it all came back to her. The push and glide, the way she could move forward with a shifting of her weight. She'd never skated on a curved surface before, or under low gravity: this was new and took some adjusting to. Gregor had obviously had some practice—he sped ahead, crossing his feet over each other like a hockey player accelerating after a puck. In a moment he was gone, hidden by the curl of ice and the false sky.

As she moved through the artificial winter, something softened inside her. Something she hadn't known was so hard and painful until it began, just a little, to melt.

Then Gregor sped past with a whoop, tagging her shoulder. She grinned at his retreating form and dug in. The ice crunched under her blades. He wasn't the only one who knew how to move quickly.

Even in low gravity, she felt her thighs burn as she chased him. It took three laps, but finally she was close enough to tag him in return. She slapped his arm as she raced past, then looked back to see him bent over, face red. She stopped and skated back to him. "A moment . . . ," he huffed. Then he was down on one knee.

She reached to take his arm.

He tried to wave her away. "I am not . . ." *Huff*. "I am not old man." *Huff*. "I do not need . . ." Then he gave in and let her help him up. He leaned heavily against her as they skated to their exit, then hobbled over to the bench.

She went to take off his skates.

"Just one moment," he said, but it took a good five minutes before his breathing returned to normal and the flush had subsided.

Saga watched the snowflakes swirl down, the slight shimmer of the projected landscape on the wall across from them. She knew if she was too sympathetic he would stiffen up, defensive, so she took off her own skates and sat quietly with him. It was an old, familiar feeling.

"Back home," Gregor said, "there would be cart with chestnuts and meat pies. Hot wine to warm our insides."

"I'm warm enough." Saga turned to face him on the bench. "Why alcohol?"

Gregor frowned. "Hot wine is good."

"Not that. I mean, why do you drink? Aren't there

more subtle ways to dull your senses? Safer ones? It just seems so old-fashioned. So . . . crude."

Gregor was quiet for a moment. "What does it matter to you?"

"In Iceland we can choose which parent we take our surname from. I'm Saga Hannesdóttir now, after my mother, but I was born Saga Ólafsdóttir."

"Ah," Gregor said. "So your father disappointed you."

She nodded slowly. "Ólafur drank. He probably still drinks. I don't know; I haven't seen him for a decade."

"And you meet me, and I drink, so you think, 'Ah, sad Russian man will provide insight into my bad father.' Is that right?"

"Forget it," Saga said. She stood up. "I'm sorry I asked."

Gregor found her hand. "Wait," he said. "Sit. Please."

She sat, grudgingly.

"I cannot tell you about your father. I know nothing of him. Only this I can say: Alcohol is old club with which to beat oneself. It has long tradition of self-destruction. A man who chooses to drink is romantic." He held up his hand at her puzzled expression. "Not in love way. Romantic in *old* way. He thinks he is noble and doomed."

"And you?" Saga said on impulse. "Are you noble and doomed?"

Gregor's expression was clouded, unreadable. "Some

mistakes we make can be forgiven. Some cannot." He took off his skates and put on his shoes. Then he stood and shuffled toward the exit. Saga followed, quiet. Halfway there he turned and looked into her eyes, a sadness in his own. "For your father, I think perhaps is your job to decide if his mistakes can be forgiven."

~

The next morning Saga received a message from her aunt. A video of her and Saga's uncle, her nieces, all sending their condolences. She felt a warmth, watching the familiar faces. It finally coaxed out the tears she hadn't cried the day before and she let them come.

Saga was working on her mother's obituary, Michel beside her, when they were interrupted by an alert that chimed from the ceiling of the room. Then the ship's voice: "The captain has asked all senior crew to report to the bridge for an emergency meeting."

When they got to the bridge, Wei had the ship's mind display open. "You need to tell me what the fuck is going on."

Saga looked at the images. "I don't see—," she started. But Michel was already frowning. He sat at a console and started typing.

"Odd," he said.

"Goddamn right it's odd," Wei said. "What are you pulling?"

Michel looked up at her, confused. "We're not pulling anything. I don't have a clue what happened."

The display looked as it always had to Saga, but then this part had long been Michel's specialty. "What?" she said. "What's wrong?"

"They're all gone," Wei said. "And nobody but the two of you had access. Goddamn Gregor wouldn't be capable, I can tell you that."

"The navigation corrections," Michel said. "Wei thinks we changed them back. But we didn't. Wei, you're the only one who's had access since we hacked the system. Look—I'll show you the logs."

"You think I trust a hacker's logs?"

Saga sat at the console beside Michel and scrolled through the system status screens. "You tried to input navigation changes?"

Wei looked at her, at Michel. Her anger lost some of its edge. "I had it all in there, ready to go. All we needed was for the reactor to come fully online. I set it up last night, but this morning the reactor was idling and the navigation instructions were gone. Like I'd never done a thing."

Michel typed furiously. He glanced back at Wei. "You did save everything after you input the commands, right?"

"Of course I fucking saved them. What sort of amateur do you think I am?"

"What sort of people do you think *we* are to go back and change things? Why would we do that?"

Wei banged her gloved hand on the console in front of her. "Don't pretend you didn't want more time here."

That was the last straw. Saga stormed over to Wei. She stood over her, glaring down at the other woman's pinched, suspicious face. "My mother is *dead,* in case you've forgotten. I don't want to explore; I just want to go home." As she said it she realized it was true. She was going back to Earth, even if it was just to visit her mother's grave and have a cry with her relatives. "Every hour here is an hour I've lost. So don't accuse us of wasting *your* time. It's insulting."

Wei glared back, then her expression changed. A brief moment of guilt or sorrow. She shut her eyes. "Okay," she said quietly. "I'm sorry about your mother. If there's anything you need to do before we leave, you should go do it now."

Saga closed down her displays. She looked at Michel. "You coming?"

He hesitated, spoke to Wei. "You want me to run you through the steps in sequence?"

Wei didn't look up. "Go. Be with your wife. I know what I'm doing. I'm going to warm up the reactor and make the course corrections and then I'm going to sit here until it actually happens."

~

Michel led Saga by the hand down the corridors. She pulled him to a stop. "I can't do the interactive," Saga said. "I've seen enough of this ship. My fans like stories set in ruins, places haunted by history." She thought of Gregor's ice rink. "The *Martian Queen* is lovely . . . in its own way, but in the end it's just an empty hotel."

"I know," Michel said.

"Then where are you leading me?"

"To the *Sigurd*." He ran a hand through his hair. "You want to make arrangements to go home, right? We're going to need the ship's comms, and access to our bank account. I'm not waiting for Wei's so-called help."

Saga felt a pulse of gratitude. She embraced him. "Thank you," she said. "But how will we get in? Wei's locked us out."

Michel smiled. "We broke into this ship. You really think she can keep us out of the *Sigurd*?"

It took twice as long to defeat Wei's overrides as it had to hack into the *Queen*. But in terms of jobs they'd done, it was barely in the middle of the pack in difficulty. Wei was no expert, and they possessed state-of-the-art intrusion gear.

Inside, supplies floated everywhere, most of them only loosely tethered to the walls. They pushed themselves carefully through the air lock and past the galley onto the bridge. Michel collided with a box of dehydrated algal protein packets and swore. The box tumbled away, bumping into a box of filters for the CO_2 scrubbers.

"*C'est le bordel*—what a mess. What has she been up to?" he said.

Saga pulled herself into one of the chairs and turned on the communication interface. "I don't care," she said. "As long as she drops us off somewhere on the way back, I'm happy to be done with her forever." She connected to the networks that spanned the solar system, requesting the status of ships bound for Earth: locations, ports of call, who was taking passengers.

The ship maintained the usual system almanac: a local copy of detailed information on ports, habitats, transport schedules, and ships in flight. But there was always drift if the almanac wasn't kept in sync with the network. From the logs, she could see that Wei hadn't updated in weeks. It was poor practice for a ship's captain. What else had she neglected?

Not for the first time, Saga cursed the speed of light. It had seemed fast enough when she lived on Earth, but out here in the rest of the solar system it was a frustrating reminder of just how far apart everything was.

Finally, data started trickling in. She closed her eyes, willing the time to pass more quickly.

"Saga, you have to see this."

She opened her eyes. Michel floated upside down above her. "I'm waiting for the schedules," she grumbled.

"Then you have time," he said. "Come on."

She sighed and unbuckled from her chair, pushing up to follow him aft to the crew quarters. He led her to Wei's cabin.

"You didn't actually break into her room?"

Michel nodded. "Don't you think we need to know what she's up to?"

"Actually we shouldn't—" Saga stopped at the cabin's entrance. "Oh my . . ."

The space was the complete opposite of the rest of the ship. They'd waded through clutter to get there, but Wei's room was like the calm center of a hurricane. Every surface gleamed, everything was packed and labeled and aligned crisply. She caught a slight smell of bleach. The room looked as if nobody had set foot in it since the ship had been launched.

The only human touch was a photograph in a hammered iron frame, hanging on the wall beside the bed. Wei with her arm around a man.

Michel was floating by the far wall. There was a high-resolution viewscreen beside him, beneath it a set of manipulator gloves.

"What is that?" Saga said, moving closer.

"There's a level-five biocontainment box attached to the outside of the hull."

Saga had seen biocontainment boxes before on medical ships. They provided crewmembers protection from the most dangerous of biological hazards. The box itself would be sealed, surrounded by vacuum outside the ship, every manipulator controlled remotely. No chance of contamination.

Michel pointed to the screen. "Can you make any sense of it?"

Saga shook her head. The screen showed the inside of the box, which held an array of everyday objects: a bar of soap with the logo of the shipping line stamped on it. A piece of wood from one of the carved doors. One of Gregor's bottles of whiskey. A loaf of bread.

"She's been testing things from the *Queen,*" Michel said.

He tapped the display panel, swiping through images. Saga recognized mass spectroscopy panels, the sort of tools miners used to evaluate the content of asteroids.

"The ship was mothballed," she said. "Don't you think it's weird that she found some bread?"

"That's not the only thing that's strange." Michel

paused at one image. "Look at that wood. It's hollow inside. There are traces of radioactive elements. And the fine scale structure, it's laminated like an oyster shell. I thought the doors were supposed to be hand-carved by artisans."

"Maybe it came from some sort of printer."

Michel rubbed his jaw thoughtfully. "Not any printer *I've* ever heard of. What is she looking for?"

Saga pushed back. Wei was a mystery that refused to be solved. She drifted past the bed, staring blankly at the framed photo across from her. There was something about the picture, something familiar.

"Oh," she said.

"What?"

"I've seen him before," Saga said, pointing. "On the *Queen*."

Beside a grinning Wei, his arm around her shoulder, was the sad man who'd appeared before her in the dining room. He was smiling here too.

It didn't make any sense. The last dinner on the *Queen* would have taken place more than twenty years ago, and the recorded party she'd witnessed was probably even older than that. But the image in front of her was recent; Wei looked the same, other than her expression. Saga realized she'd never seen Wei smile.

Michel peered at the photograph. "How the hell did

you see—" He stopped and touched his earbud, answering a call. "We're exploring, Wei. Like you said." He made a face. "Fine, we'll look for him." He ended the call and grimaced. "She wants us to dig up Gregor. She thinks he can help with the nav, but he's not responding to messages."

"Tell her to wait," Saga said. "Tell her we're here and she's not locking us out again."

Michel shook his head. "I don't want her to know we came aboard, okay? Not yet. Whatever she's got going on, it's more than just adjusting the *Queen*'s orbit. This biocontainment gear costs more than she's paying us for this whole trip."

Saga looked back toward the bridge. "Fine. But I can't leave now. I'm in the middle of something."

Michel was already heading to the doorway. "Why don't you just set up a remote gateway to the *Sigurd* now that you have access to comms?"

She folded her arms, put on a stubborn expression. "You can handle Gregor," she said. "I'm staying here."

~

Saga reviewed the data. It wasn't going to be easy, but she'd found a way they could get back to Earth in fewer than fifty days. Wei would have to agree to a burn that would take them away from the *Sigurd*'s home port of Ceres. It wasn't going to be cheap, either. Wei would have to be compensated, and the ship that would take them the rest of the way would surely charge a premium.

But she would be home.

The cold wind off the ocean. The smell of the sea. She remembered taking a trip on the ring road with her mother when she was young. They'd tramped through drizzle, been briefly stranded by a snowstorm in a cozy café with a fire and a mellow dog she'd wanted to take home. A blessed week away from her father and their fighting. Only later did she realize that her mother had been trying to leave him. There had been far more than a week's worth of luggage in the car they'd rented. But her mother had failed. She'd never forget that sinking feeling when the car dropped them off in front of their little house in Breiðholt and drove itself away.

What would their lives have been like if they'd kept on going?

An alarm sounded, startlingly loud. Michel's personal emergency beacon, set to the highest level of urgency they'd ever used on an exploration. The sort of thing you'd trigger if your suit was holed or you'd discovered a leaking reactor.

She was heading for the lock before she was aware she'd unbuckled and pushed off from the chair.

Saga flew through the zero-gravity sections of the *Queen,* making tiny course corrections with her hands. She'd played games like this when she'd first arrived in the belt. Fastest through a space, smoothest trajectory. Try to get from one end of a habitat to another without touching anything. Now, she would have lost all of them but the speed contest; she slapped bulkheads, hit the edge of a door with her shoulder hard enough to leave a bruise, flapped awkwardly through the air in her rush to reach her husband.

When she entered the spin module she hit the ground running, shrugging off the dizzy transition to gravity. In her lenses she could see the blinking dot of Michel's location. The dot hadn't moved since the alarm had sounded, and he hadn't responded to any messages.

The system showed Michel in a medical station near the casino. Past the game tables and the curtains, the machinery of theater, there was a row of doors; the one nearest to her was open a crack, light spilling out. She entered and stopped short, confused. A naked woman, facedown on an examination table, a tumble of long brown hair. Beneath her, a naked man.

Neither of them was moving.

She felt weak for a moment, then Michel came into the room and she almost cried out in relief.

"You didn't answer. I thought . . ."

He looked down, a flicker of guilt on his face. "I'm sorry. I didn't want to use the comms. I wanted to talk to you first—before we told Wei."

Saga stepped forward. The man on the table was Gregor. His eyes were fixed and staring, his face caught in a surprised expression.

They were surrounded by stainless-steel cabinets and drawers, some of them open. There was a portable health monitor on one of the cabinets. Michel touched the diagnosis screen, which was blank. "Battery's dead," he said. "But I figure it was a heart attack. You know, right in the middle . . ." He looked over at Gregor.

The pilot's damp hair was stuck in tendrils to his forehead. Saga remembered how he'd huffed and puffed and nearly collapsed on the ice. He'd been in terrible shape. Why hadn't she told him to get himself checked?

"Did you try calling the *Queen*? Maybe it has emergency medical. Maybe it's not too late . . ."

Michel shook his head. "Medical is offline. They removed most of the equipment when they mothballed it. There's hardly anything in here. But I would have told you to bring supplies from the *Sigurd* if there was any hope. This happened hours ago; it's too late for him."

"Oh Gregor," she said sadly. "You foolish man."

Saga looked at the woman. She'd never seen her before. Her skin had none of Gregor's pallor or slackness.

Who *was* she? Saga reached out and touched her leg. It was smooth. No hairs, no imperfections, not even any visible pores. Then she understood. "The dancers from the brochure."

Michel nodded. "Gregor was right, they're synthetic. He took this one out of storage and activated her. Apparently he knew how to turn on some hidden features."

"I'm sure he did," Saga said. "Was she on when you arrived?"

Michel grimaced. "She was activated, but she was just lying there moaning. I turned her off."

Saga put her hand on her husband's shoulder. "We should clean him up before we call Wei."

Michel looked unsure. "We don't want it to look like we're hiding anything. Wei's paranoid enough as it is."

"I don't care. Gregor was part of our crew. He deserves a little dignity at the end."

$\sim$

Wei stood in the med station and looked at their dead pilot. Before she arrived, Saga and Michel had put Gregor's underwear back on him and carried the synth out, depositing her back in storage, where she joined a line of her companions, laid out in racks like in a morgue.

Wei's expression was guarded, her arms crossed tightly

over her chest. "We have to eject him," she said finally.

"What?" Michel looked startled.

"It's the only way to be sure."

Saga frowned at her. "Be sure of *what*?"

"That we're safe."

"From his heart attack?" Saga said. "No. We're taking his body back to his family. We can put him in the cargo hold. It's cold enough."

"Not on my ship," Wei said. "No way he's coming with us. No way."

"That's it." Saga stood in front of Wei. "Enough of this bullshit. We saw your biocontainment box. Now you're going to tell us what the fuck is going on."

Wei was startled. She looked at the two of them, comprehension slowly dawning on her. Then anger. "You got back on the *Sigurd*," she said. "You broke into my fucking ship. You invaded my *room*."

Saga shook her head. "We have a *right* to be there just as much as you do. You can't hide anything any longer. We deserve to know what you're doing."

"I'm doing my *job*," Wei said. "Moving this liner out of the way. That's all." She looked at Gregor and sighed. "If you don't want to space him, you can store him on the *Queen*. In a locked room. We're not going anywhere soon, in any case."

Michel was covering Gregor's body with a blanket.

He looked up, surprised. "I thought you said you'd have everything done in a few hours."

"So did I," Wei said.

~

They put Gregor in a cold storage locker in the main galley, after carrying him awkwardly through the corridors wrapped in the blanket. Wei secured the locker door and then the galley doors, ignoring their questions. She wouldn't say what she'd been doing in her room, or with the biocontainment box. But she *did* tell them about the problems she had been having with the *Queen*. Twice she'd tried to change course. The reactor would warm up, she would input the course corrections, hydrogen would flow, and then everything would reset, all her changes wiped out.

"It's obvious," Michel said. "There's a fail-safe in there somewhere. It's detecting your changes and rebooting to an earlier configuration."

They were back on the *Queen*'s bridge. Mind-state diagrams filled the holographic display between them. "If it's so goddamn obvious then why did you miss it?" Wei said. "Show me this fail-safe."

Saga watched Michel lose himself in the challenge. He had a remarkable ability to ignore the outside world when he was coding. But she couldn't concentrate—not after what had just happened.

Two deaths: first her mother, then Gregor. Bad fortune came in threes. Something her mother had firmly believed and she half believed herself. Saga couldn't shake the feeling that there would have to be another death. That it was coming due.

She'd lost crew before. It had been nine years ago, shortly after she arrived in the belt and before she met Michel. She'd been an intern on a salvage crew, most junior of them all. They were stripping the *Entangled Photon,* a research ship that had been holed by a chunk of ice out past Jupiter. It was a hell of a start—still the most challenging wreck she'd ever explored: tumbling and spinning rapidly, it was treacherous inside. Jagged metal punctured the suit of one of the other explorers in their group, a woman named Nadira, and she panicked and got entangled in a mess of wiring. A water line ruptured above her suit's pressure cuff and the ship's wild spin filled her helmet with liquid. She'd drowned before anyone could get to her, dead beyond all hope of recovery.

Saga stayed with Nadira's body until they could move it safely. Afterward she'd created a virtual memorial, an interactive model of the wreck, with Nadira hanging in the center like a lost angel, surrounded by the voices of her friends and family talking about her life. It had been the beginning of Saga's artistic career; it had given her a reputation, though she'd never felt entirely comfortable with the thought that someone else's sacrifice had put her on the road to her success.

Maybe Nadira had been the first death. Maybe Gregor was the third, and the fates were now satisfied. It would be nice to believe that, but she knew the universe rarely operated the way you wanted it to.

"There," Michel said.

Saga pulled herself away from the memory of the young woman's face, distorted by the water in her helmet.

Wei squinted. "There *what*?"

Michel adjusted the display. Mind-system maps faded to reveal what looked like the skeleton of a leaf: an organic tracery of silvery lines shimmering in the space in the center of the room.

Saga stared at the pattern. "Subtractive overlay?"

Michel shook his head, thoughtful. "Onion-skin algorithm, actually. You get better temporal resolution."

"In English, please," Wei snapped.

"It's a map," Michel said. "The AI is riddled with hidden code. It's a type of neural network that isn't in the original mind's programming. I only found it when I split the code into layers and started moving through them, minimizing everything that was supposed to be there."

"Could it be a virus?" Saga said.

Michel shrugged. "Whatever it is, it seems to be growing. It's already one percent larger than it was an hour ago. Maybe turning on the ship's mind woke it up."

"A ghost in the machine," Saga said. Like something half glimpsed in a mirror. Like the man she'd seen in the dining room, Wei's man. Yet another mystery their employer was keeping to herself.

"It's preventing the course change?" Wei waved her hand, signaling for their attention.

Michel nodded. "Looks like it."

"Then turn it off. Edit it out."

Michel stared into space, viewing readouts that only he could see. "Problem is, the map isn't the territory. We're just looking at my best guess at what's there. It's a different story to go in and try to change something that's embedded that deep without damaging anything. Do you have any idea how complex a ship's mind is?"

"I don't care about the fucking details. Just do it." Wei's face was flushed, her gloved hands opening and closing.

It took three more hours to find a work-around. Wei insisted that none of them leave. Saga kept Michel hydrated, fed him a protein bar when he looked like he needed it, made comments when she had something useful to say. But this deep expedition into the code was his.

The final result was messy, inelegant. Michel had no hope of teasing out all the unusual code, so instead he put parts of the ship's mind back to sleep. He kept the motor areas—the attitude and drive controls—awake. To access this partial mind he created a simple interface, more plumbing than programming. They would use the *Sigurd*'s computer to control the burn.

Wei did the work on the *Sigurd*'s systems, refusing Michel's and Saga's offers to help her. When everything was ready, Wei brought the reactor up to full strength. She opened the propellant valves. The liner rumbled and they all felt the gentle, growing push of acceleration as the *Martian Queen* began to change course.

"I need a break," Michel said, stretching his back. "I have to move."

"Go ahead," Wei said. "I'll message you if I need anything."

~

They were both exhausted. Saga had a long shower; when she got out Michel was sprawled on the bed, snoring gently. She lay beside him. She would close her eyes, but only for a moment.

Saga woke with a start when she felt something damp on her face. Her hair was going to be a mess. As she reached for her towel, something nagged at her. She picked up the towel and let it go, then watched as it fell slowly, taking a slightly curved path to the floor.

"Michel," she said. She shoved his shoulder.

"Mmm," he grumbled.

"We're still under thrust."

He pushed himself up on his elbows. "That's odd, it's been . . ." He paused, checking his implant. "Merde, it's been nearly three hours. Why is Wei still running the engines?"

When they got to the bridge, they found Wei at the console. She might not have moved since they left her.

"What the hell, Wei?" Saga said. "This is no minor course correction."

"Change of plans."

Saga looked at Michel, who was gazing, unfocused, at a point over her shoulder. Calculating something. After a minute he made eye contact. "We're moving too fast for a simple orbit change," he said. "We reached solar system escape velocity a few minutes ago."

"*Fokk*," Saga swore. Wei had just ruined their travel plans back to Earth. "What is this?"

"What needs to be done." Wei tapped the console and the engines turned off. They all swayed slightly with the loss of acceleration. "There," she said. "Good enough." She touched the control interfaces, and readouts around the room shifted.

Michel looked confused. "What are you shutting down?"

"All of it: the reactor, the ship's mind, the life support."

"We never agreed to that," Saga said. She thought of the carved doors cracking, water freezing, and pipes bursting.

"You had your time," Wei said. "The job's done now. You're going to want to suit up soon if you enjoy breathing."

"*Helvítis bjáni,*" Saga spat, the English words failing her. "You're going to wreck the *Queen.*"

Wei ignored her. Status lights switched from green to amber all over the display.

"They're in the room, Saga," Michel said. She looked at him blankly. "Our suits. We left them in the room."

"So?"

"Wei's shutting down life support. We need to get our suits on."

Saga glared at Wei, who continued to ignore her. She looked at Michel, saw the urgency on his face. She took a long breath, trying to calm herself.

"Okay," she said. "Let's go."

~

They pulled on their suits quickly. Michel fumbled with one of his gloves. Saga reached over and adjusted the stuck bearing that had prevented a proper seal. "You have some sort of plan?"

"Yeah," he said. "We get the hell out of here and go home."

Saga picked up her helmet. "That's it?"

Michel closed his eyes for a moment. He looked tired. "What do you want, Saga? You want to pick a fight with Wei, who has control of the ship and is shutting down life support? You want to stay on this empty liner? You were the one who was so desperate to return to Earth." He paused for a second. "Look, the sooner we do this, the sooner we can start back."

Saga winced. "Yes . . . Yes, of course." She sighed. "We have to take Gregor's body with us. If Wei's so damn worried, she can put him in her fancy biocontainment box. But we have to do the right thing by him."

"I know," Michel said. "He was crew. We owe him that."

They packed their few things. Saga slipped the black dress into the thigh pouch on her suit. Michel carried her video and mapping gear. They walked through the ship, heading for the galley. Halfway there an alarm sounded and the rotational force that had provided the sensation of Mars gravity dropped away.

"She wasn't kidding about shutting everything off," Michel said over the suit comm.

Saga looked at the environment display in her suit. It showed the temperature and air pressure dropping steadily. "She's crazy. What if we hadn't made it to the room?"

Wei's voice sounded in their helmets. "Come now. I have camera control and I can see your data readouts. I knew you were suited up."

"And comm access," Michel grunted.

"Obviously." A pause. "I know you're going for his body. Don't. Nothing from the ship comes back."

Saga looked at Michel. An understanding passed between them. They were going to get Gregor anyway. She didn't care what Wei wanted anymore. They continued through the doors marked *Staff Access Only,* pushing themselves toward the main galley.

Michel stopped short in the open doorway, and Saga collided with him. He lost his grip and they both tumbled into the galley.

It took a moment to get themselves straightened out. Over the comm Saga could hear her husband's breathing, muttered curses. Then she saw why.

The door to the cold storage locker they'd put Gregor in was wide open. The locker was empty.

"Wei?" Michel mouthed.

Saga nodded. She must have dumped the body already. This was beyond caution; something had to be wrong with Wei. Some deep pathology. Would she even let them back on the *Sigurd*? Would they have to fight her?

There was a stirring in the air. A vibration swept through the ship. If she hadn't been holding on to the door frame with her hand she might not have noticed it. Saga felt her body being drawn aft.

"We're under acceleration," she said. "Wei, can you hear us? What are you doing?"

"We can't be." Wei's voice was strained. "The reactor's offline. The drive isn't on. Don't move." A wobble in the last word.

Michel caught her attention. There was a window in the galley door. As the ship's temperature dropped, frost had formed. He quickly wrote on the glass: *Where to? Bridge or Sigurd? Or?*

Saga pointed to the *Sigurd*. Michel nodded.

~

They were almost to the service bay when Wei contacted them over the comm. "I need your help."

Saga shook her head. "Screw you, Wei. You spaced Gregor."

"I wish I had. You're not going to believe this."

"Why should we believe anything you say?"

Michel went ahead to open the service hatch, but it wouldn't respond to the code they'd programmed in. Their previous hack was gone. He swore and kicked the hatch, floating backward toward Saga.

She pushed off the wall and snagged him as he came by.

"Unlock the fucking hatch, Wei," Michel said.

Silence. Finally Wei replied, "I can't. The ship won't respond." Wei swore. "Oh just look for yourselves."

A screen on the wall next to the hatch blinked to life, showing the exterior of the *Queen*. The familiar shape of the *Sigurd* was there, as expected. What wasn't expected was the blue glow of her main drive, a flood of energetic particles lighting up the darkness behind her. The image switched to show Gregor in his pilot's chair. He sat still, staring blankly ahead, only wearing the underwear they'd put on him when they found him.

"Oh my God," Saga said. "He's still alive." She touched the screen, as if the image would vanish. Instead she could feel a steady vibration.

"Find a way to stop him," Wei said. "He's changing our course back."

"Didn't you contact him? What did he say?"

"Of course I tried to fucking contact him. He's not responding. Just do something."

Saga looked at Michel, his wide, surprised eyes. She was sure she looked the same. "You're going to have to do it, Michel," she said. "You have the gear."

"Okay," he said. "What do I do first, open the lock?"

"Get control of the ship's systems. Turn the engine off," Wei said. "Then we'll figure out the next step."

Michel tethered himself to the wall by the hatch. Saga watched as he closed his eyes, saw the twitches of his fingers as he entered the virtual space of the intrusion software.

Saga tried to puzzle everything out: Wei's odd behavior, the reappearance of Gregor, his actions on the *Sigurd*. Gregor must have woken from some sort of deep unconsciousness and found a safety lock release inside the storage area. What would it have been like to wake in the cold and dark like that? But it still didn't explain why he would go to the *Sigurd* and fire up the engines. Unless he was trying to leave.

She stared at the screen. Containers moved behind Gregor, all drifting in the same direction as the thrust from the *Sigurd*'s main drive pushed both ships. His face was pale and waxy. No expression. He reached out mechanically and touched a control, then returned his hand to his lap. "He hasn't blinked," she said after a minute. "Not since I've been watching. Something's wrong with him."

"Shit," Michel said. "The *Sigurd*'s engine controls are manually locked out."

"Wei," Saga said over the comm. "Are you seeing this?"

"Just deal with it, Saga. I don't care how. He's burning

hard. He's using up our propellant. If he keeps this up, we won't have enough left to get anywhere."

"Anything, Michel?" Saga said.

"I have low-level access," he said. "But nothing useful. I can't access propulsion or navigation."

"Can you access environmental controls?"

"No."

Something occurred to her. "What about emergency systems? Fire suppression?"

A pause from Michel. "Yes," he finally said. "We have that." He blinked at her with alarm. "You really want to suffocate him?"

"Just temporarily. If we make him lose consciousness, we can flush the atmosphere, right? Bring it back to normal. No harm done."

"Maybe some harm," Michel said hesitantly. "None of us are doctors."

"How are we for propellant?"

He paused again. She could see he was afraid. Well, so was she, but they had to act.

"What are you waiting for?" Wei said. "Just do it! He's already dropped our velocity by two kilometers per second. The engine's running over one hundred percent load. If he keeps it up we're totally screwed."

Saga nodded at Michel. "Go."

On the screen, warning lights strobed in the cabin.

Then a billow of fog as the cold nitrogen of the fire suppression system flooded the room. Gregor faded to a shadow on the screen, a statue shrouded by mist. A minute later everything was clear again as powerful fans pulled the gas from the room.

Gregor sat at the pilot's station, unblinking. Unchanged. He reached forward and touched the control surface.

"That's impossible," Michel said. "There was no breathable air in there."

Saga felt the vibration through the wall, a ragged syncopation. "What did he just do?"

"Emergency thrust," Michel said. "He's overridden all the safeties."

"Get away from the hatch," Wei yelled. Her voice was distorted, almost unrecognizable.

"Why?" Saga said. "What are you going to do?"

"Not me: *him*. There are alarms all over the board. The hull's failing. Get out of there."

Michel was still tethered to the wall. She grabbed him, then unclipped and pushed off in a fluid motion. They were floating back toward the service-bay doors when the wall around the docking port ripped apart.

The noise was a hammer. Saga felt it in her bones. Decompression alarms wailed, then rapidly faded to silence as air rushed from the cargo area. Flashing red lights.

Emergency doors sealed. Beyond the destroyed hatch stretched the black fabric of space, punctured by a landscape of stars. The force of escaping air had counteracted their movement, and they slowly drifted back toward the hole where the port had been. Saga watched over Michel's shoulder as the *Sigurd* tumbled away, engine still flaring.

The silence was broken by the sound of her gasping breath.

~

They understood the situation they were in only later, after Wei had sealed and evacuated the cargo compartment behind the service bay, allowing them to get through the emergency doors. After they had made their way, stunned, up to the *Queen*'s bridge, where Wei had shown them footage from the ship's cameras.

The docking port had been ripped from the ship under the *Sigurd*'s emergency thrust. It shouldn't have; it was rated for far more stress than it had taken. But the hull around it had crumbled, the metal strangely fragile, almost hollowed out. Afterward, the *Sigurd* had tumbled and spun, engine still firing. It was heading directly toward the *Queen* when the liner's anticollision systems had engaged.

The systems were designed to vaporize fast-moving fragments of rock and ice or push larger objects out of the way. They made short work of the *Sigurd*. The footage showed the sparks of pusher drones: chemical rockets that connected themselves to the ship's hull and fired to slow it. Next, powerful lasers had made the metal of the *Sigurd*'s hull glow yellow. Although its momentum had been reduced by the drones, the half-melted ship had still made contact with the *Queen* and was now fused to the hull, a warty growth on the liner's sleek side.

It had been their way home. Now it was slag.

Saga couldn't pull herself away from the footage, puzzled and horrified in equal measure. One of the cameras had captured the moment the ship split apart, ripping like paper as a glowing dot traced its side. A half-shadowed body had tumbled out before being pinned in laser light like an insect under a magnifying glass. Gregor had boiled away into space under the ferocious heat of the ship's defenses.

Saga rewound and watched again, confused. The corpse was no threat to the ship. It shouldn't have noticed him. Yet during a moment when the *Sigurd* was still on a collision course with the *Queen*, the lasers had focused on his body instead. They'd allowed the ship to collide with the *Queen* rather than ignore Gregor. It didn't make sense.

"So I guess we're going to get caught," Michel grumbled, interrupting her musing. "No sneaking home now. Any port we take the *Queen* to, they're going to make a fuss."

Wei's faceplate had been dark as she sat brooding. Now it flickered on, revealing her expression. She looked shaken. "No port," she said. "No port. It doesn't matter. There's only one thing left to do."

"What thing?" Saga said. But Wei just dimmed her faceplate and became silent again.

She was useless; they'd just have to route around her.

Saga stood up. Wei had reversed the shutdown procedure. Gravity had returned. Her suit showed normal temperature and pressure in the room. It also showed she'd depleted half its oxygen and power. She stripped it off. Watching her, Michel did the same. "I'll search the ship for supplies," she said to him. "If we're going to be here a while, we need to know what we have."

"I'll come with you."

She shook her head, then tilted it at Wei. *Keep an eye on her.* "Why don't you stay and run some numbers? We need to know how much propellant is left, how long it will take us to get back to civilization."

Michel nodded. "Of course." He sat down at his console and a work space opened up in front of him. When Saga left, he was deep in orbital calculations.

~

Saga went back to the casino. The melancholy space felt even emptier than before, now that Gregor was gone. She checked behind the bar and found the water dispenser and a small sink. A food printer that was empty and offline. Rows of glasses and neatly folded bar towels. A box of drink coasters with the *Martian Queen*'s logo. She touched one and a small image of the liner slid slowly across its face.

There was a clatter from backstage. Startled, Saga looked toward the curtain. She heard a tapping sound, getting louder. "Wei?" she said. "Michel?" No response. She couldn't help imagining Gregor's shuffling corpse, burnt to a cinder.

Tap tap tap. With a click the curtains opened, revealing a lone figure at the center of the stage. Saga's heart hammered in her chest. The figure bowed low, a cascade of brown hair tumbling down as she did.

Saga let out her breath. It was the woman who'd been with Gregor. The synth dancer. She was wearing black high heels, stockings, and a red dress that artfully revealed slightly more than it concealed. She had very long legs. She lifted her head and looked Saga in the eyes.

"May I dance for you?" she said, her voice like honey.

Saga had experience with humanoid synthetics before; they were useful in dangerous environments and did much of the unpleasant work in the belt. But they were designed to be clearly artificial. Form following function. Until now, she'd never met one so eerily lifelike.

"Perhaps I could sing for you instead?" the synth said.

Saga shook her head. "No. No thank you."

The synth nodded and relaxed her pose. She walked to the front of the stage and stepped down. She came smiling toward Saga, who found herself backing away until she bumped into the wall of shelving behind her.

"May I get you a refreshment?" The synth now spoke with the voice of the ship. "Something to eat?"

"Sure," Saga said, wanting to get away from this uncanny machine. "Go get me something to eat."

"Would you care to see the menu?"

"No. Just . . . anything. A steak sandwich. Fetch me one of those."

The synth nodded. "Of course, madam. Anything else?"

For a moment Saga imagined her returning with an actual steak sandwich, conjured up from some secret store of luxuries. They could travel back to Earth in comfort, like on a real cruise. But that was ridiculous.

The synth stood, waiting. Her hair gleamed in the room lights. Her chest rose and fell as she breathed. Dark, liquid eyes flickered in tiny movements. *Saccades:*

that was the word. An imitation of life.

"Do you have a name?" Saga asked.

The synth smiled. "Krasivaya. It is Russian for 'beautiful.'"

"Did Gregor give you that name?"

The synth tilted her head slightly. "I don't understand the question."

"You can go now, Krasivaya," Saga said. "I'd like to be alone."

"Of course, madam."

The synth turned and walked back across the room and onto the stage, vanishing behind the curtain.

Saga left the casino and took corridors at random until she found herself heading back toward the presidential suite. Her and Michel's home while they worked out how to get to their real home.

She stopped. There was no guarantee they would return, was there? They were going to have to start thinking seriously about survival: all their food had been on the *Sigurd*. She tried to remember the data she'd requested when she was searching for a way back to Earth. The *Sigurd* had generated a list of the various ships traveling in the region of space they occupied. There hadn't been many, and the nearest was many millions of kilometers away and moving in the opposite direction.

Every so often she was reminded of the sheer vastness

of the solar system. How the maps and schedules they relied on focused on the tiny islands of light people had created out there. In reality, it was almost entirely empty space. Blackness in all directions.

"Ship," she said. "Are you there?"

"How may I help you?" the ship's voice replied.

"Gregor's room. Which one was it?"

"I'm sorry," the ship said. "I don't have a passenger manifest for this voyage."

She thought for a second. "There were two rooms occupied recently. One of them was the presidential suite. Could you tell me which one the other guest stayed in?"

"Of course," the ship said. "Just follow the yellow line on the wall."

A warm glow lit the corridor.

~

Entering Gregor's room, Saga felt a wave of memory overtake her. It was the smell more than anything, stale sweat and alcohol. She could have been back in her family's house again. She put her hand on the door frame and closed her eyes. She couldn't go in.

She'd spent the last half of her teenage years in Germany with a loose coalition of urban explorers, living on Guaranteed Income and taking trains around Europe to break into various abandoned factories and government facilities left over from the second industrial revolution. It had been a good life, while it lasted. Then one day she'd received a message from her aunt: her mother had been hospitalized.

When she returned to Iceland she found a house gone to seed, an eerie mirror of the run-down places she'd been exploring. The house mind was unresponsive. The cleaning systems had malfunctioned months before and had never been fixed. There were balls of fluff under the beds. Fragments of food littered the kitchen floor and countertops.

Her anxiety lived in her stomach those days. A corrosive drip of worry, anger, and guilt. She walked around the familiar rooms while she tried to imagine how it had been. After all her mother's threats and failed attempts to leave, it was her father who had finally been the one to go. Her mother had withdrawn from the world afterward, sunk into a depression. After months of solitude she'd had an aneurysm. She'd been undiscovered for days. Certainly her daughter had nothing to do with finding her: Saga hadn't called her for months.

Saga stayed in the house for six weeks, scrubbing it clean centimeter by centimeter between trips to the hospital. She blamed herself. She blamed her father. She permanently locked him out of every personal and social system she had control of, but he still showed up one day on the doorstep, wanting to talk. He told her he'd gone to rehab. He was a new man and he wanted to see his daughter.

She'd hidden inside, shaking. Not with fear, but with anger, and the realization that if she opened the door she might try to kill him.

A month later, after it became clear her mother wasn't going to get better, Saga fled Earth to seek her fortune in the belt and to start trying to pay back what she owed.

Now here she was, the woman who left. The woman who'd caused her mother's death. Stuck in a doorway by the smell of stale booze.

She opened her eyes and forced herself forward. On the floor was a tangle of clothing, Gregor's pressure suit crammed under the bed. She nudged aside an empty bottle with her foot.

There was also food. Gregor had taken more than his share from the rations Wei had left for them after she'd locked them out of the *Sigurd*. She could bring that back, at least. They were going to need it. The full bottles of liquor—and there were still several of those lined up on the dresser—she left untouched. They may have contained calories, but nobody needed the pain they held.

On the desk sat a partially eaten loaf of bread. It looked the same as the one Wei had been examining on the *Sigurd*. Saga touched it gingerly, then picked it up. The flour-dusted loaf looked like it had come from a wood-fired oven, and it felt like bread, more or less. Hard crust, like the real thing. She sniffed it, but it had no scent.

"Would you like to eat here, madam?"

Saga dropped the bread and spun around, her arms held out to ward off whoever had spoken. Just outside the doorway was a man in a crisp uniform. He wore a white apron and held a dish with a silver cover, a white linen towel draped over his arm. He stood there, neat as a pin, waiting for her response.

He had to be another synth, she realized. The voice he'd spoken with was that of the ship.

"*Fokking helvíti,*" Saga swore. "Don't sneak up on people like that."

"I apologize. I *did* announce myself."

"Well, I didn't hear you." She took a breath and looked at the dish. "What's that?"

The synth removed the cover. Under it was a steak sandwich and what looked like a mound of mashed potatoes. "Your food," the synth said. "I can clear a space for you at the desk."

"No," Saga said after a stunned moment. "Not in here. This room needs a good cleaning. We'll go next door."

The room was immaculate and empty, the bed bare

of coverings and the closet doors wide open. The synth placed the dish on the desk, then laid out a napkin and a knife and fork, producing salt and pepper shakers from a pocket in his uniform. He arranged everything carefully, then stepped back. "May I get you anything else?"

Saga shook her head. She watched as he turned and left without a sound, then leaned forward and sniffed cautiously at the meal. The sandwich smelled like nothing, like Gregor's loaf of bread. She reached out and touched it, then held it up to her eyes. From a distance it looked entirely convincing—there were even grill marks on the bread—but up close the illusion broke down and the lie of it was revealed.

∽

Michel was fascinated by the sandwich. He sniffed it, as Saga had done. Hefted it. "You didn't take a bite?"

Saga shook her head. "Does it look edible to you?"

"Sure, more or less."

"But it's obviously not *actual* food. It's like the ship knows what food looks like, but it doesn't know anything else about it."

Michel put the sandwich down on the console beside him. When Saga had returned, she'd found her husband deep in data. He hadn't even realized that Wei had left the bridge. He gestured at an image of the ship's mind. The tracery of foreign code they'd found earlier glowed, brighter than before. "I wonder if it's connected to that code. Maybe the food printers have been reprogrammed by it."

"I searched the galleys," Saga said. "There's nothing there. All the food printer tanks were empty. The algal plant was offline. The cupboards are bare."

He picked up the sandwich again. "Yet here it is. I did the calculations. You already found out there were no ships nearby, and it's going to take us a long time to get anywhere. Weeks and weeks at the minimum. It would be nice if this was edible." He frowned. "Food is just molecules: amino acids, proteins. The ship should know about calories and nutrition. Maybe it created this from the maintenance printer feedstock. We could eat it, even if it doesn't have any flavor. You said Gregor was eating the bread, right?"

He lifted the sandwich to his mouth. Saga suddenly felt afraid. "Michel, don't."

One moment Wei was a flicker coming up the stairs, the next she'd knocked the sandwich from Michel's hand and planted herself between them.

"*Putain!*" Michel swore. He rubbed his right hand.

"Did you eat any of it?" Wei said.

Michel scowled at her. "What?"

"Did you eat any?" she yelled. "Any of the ship's food?" She turned around to face Saga, her eyes wild. "Did *you*?"

"No," Saga said. She held both hands up defensively. "Neither of us did! What the hell is going on?"

Wei held out an open package. Saga looked at it. It was full of emergency rations. Inside were a dozen or so tan bricks—nutritional bars, each with a day's worth of calories, protein, and fat. Shelf-stable for decades. Every ship had a few containers stuffed in a locker somewhere.

"None of the food is edible." Wei shook the package at her. "Not even these."

Saga took out a bar, turned it over, and found the expiration date. "It says it's still good for another ten years."

Michel took another bar. "Same here."

"Look closer," Wei said.

The bars were all the same basic ingredients, varying only by flavor: curry, hot and sour, Cajun spice. The best Saga could say about them was that they were palatable. She'd eaten a few before and regretted it. But this one had no odor.

Michel dug a finger into his. "It's like rubber . . ."

Wei snatched Saga's bar and squeezed it with her powered glove. It popped, splitting open to reveal a hollow interior. She let it fall to the floor.

Saga stared at her. "You're not surprised, are you."

Wei stared back, defiant. "I thought it might be in the

air as well, but you two seem unaffected."

Michel sniffed cautiously. "*What* was in the air?"

"Whatever took over this ship," Wei said.

"*We* did that," Michel said. "It's been mothballed for twenty years. We were the first people here."

Wei shook her head. "Something came here before us. This ship has been compromised. It's being hollowed out like these emergency rations, piece by piece."

"All the diagnostics were fine when we boarded," Michel said. "The *Queen* has a working mind and an active reactor. We stayed in the presidential suite. Everything's normal."

Wei spread her arms. "This all *looks* normal. That's the point. But the *Martian Queen* is as false as that sandwich."

Michel tossed his ration bar from hand to hand. "I'm not buying it, Wei. You know how much work it would be to strip everything out and replace it? Who would even bother?"

"I don't know," Wei said. "I thought it was a nanotech experiment gone wrong. I tried to pin down the problem with the equipment on the *Sigurd*, but I failed. What I do know is that it's dangerous, and it's in the food."

"How?" Saga said. "How do you know that?"

"Look what happened to Gregor."

Poor Gregor. They'd failed him. "He wasn't dead;

maybe he was in a coma." But as Saga said it she knew how unlikely it sounded.

"By the time we put him in cold storage, rigor mortis had set in," Wei said. "No coma does that. It's biologically impossible."

"Then what—the ship zombified him? That's *less* impossible?"

Wei just looked at her.

"Oh God." Saga turned to Michel. "Please give me a rational explanation. There must be one."

Michel regarded Wei like a dangerous animal. He dropped the bar. "Someone opened the locker and put his body onto the *Sigurd*. We know there are active synths on board. What if *they* moved him? Maybe Wei got them to do it, if she didn't do it herself."

Wei's laugh had a ragged edge to it. "You saw the video from the bridge, just like I did. Gregor was moving around by himself. There was no synth pulling his strings. And why would I destroy the *Sigurd*?"

"Okay, Wei," Saga said. "You know so much, you tell us. What happened to him? What exactly did the food do?"

"It turned him into something else. Something . . . alien."

"How the hell do you know that?"

Wei reached up and slowly unlatched her helmet. It

came off with a slight hiss of escaping air. She blinked, took a cautious breath. It was the first time they'd seen her bare face in days. She looked at both of them. "I have a story to tell you."

~

It wasn't Wei's first visit to the *Queen*.

Three years earlier she'd been there with her partner, Ayanti. The two of them were running unauthorized salvage trips, traveling dark, plundering what they could from wrecks and abandoned facilities. Even, she admitted, sometimes stealing from automated mining stations and habitats under construction.

He was the hacker, she the salvage expert, identifying valuable technology, artifacts, minerals, anything worth the fuel and time to take back to the black marketers.

They used the same intrusion package she'd brought on this trip to break through the *Queen*'s defenses. Inside they found a treasure trove. They cut out carvings, took plates and silverware, piled up fittings and furniture. Their cargo nets were crammed full.

"Near the end we got into the alcohol," she said. Wei paused and Saga could see regret and pain in her eyes. "That's when it all began."

They partied in the presidential suite, celebrating their

good fortune and impending wealth. Drank more than they should have. The last thing she remembered was Ayanti ordering room service, laughing. When she woke, hungover, late the next day, Ayanti wasn't there. She discovered the room-service meal had been delivered, after all, and Ayanti had eaten it. She went to their ship, looking for him, and found their cargo nets and pressurized containers empty.

On the *Queen*, every single thing they'd taken had been returned to its proper place.

Throughout the liner there was an oppressive silence. Until she reached the doors to the dining room. "I got there," she said. "And I heard it. The sounds of a dinner party. Clinking forks, conversation, laughter. God, I even heard that string quartet—" She broke off, her eyes closed.

She hammered on the doors, but they wouldn't open. When she finally broke in, the diners vanished. "All except for Ayanti," she said. "He was sitting at a table, dressed in a tuxedo, eating a steak. When I touched him he looked at me . . ." Wei wiped her nose on the back of her glove. "But he didn't really see me."

He talked to her as if they were guests on the ship, as if the *Queen* were full of passengers sailing to Mars. He told her about the people he'd eaten with, shared their gossip.

She put it down to stress and exhaustion, assuming

he'd returned everything in a fit of guilt. Somehow he'd fixed the damage they'd done, or triggered the ship's self-repair protocols.

Hoping sleep would help, she brought him back to their suite and sedated him, locking him in. She spent a day reassembling their haul, refilling the cargo nets and containers with things she could take by herself. When she returned to the suite he was gone.

She searched the *Queen,* but he wasn't on board.

"I found him outside," Wei said. "Without his pressure suit. He was in vacuum—in his fucking tuxedo, ripping apart the cargo nets with his bare hands."

Wei was quiet for a long moment. "I suited up and grabbed him. I don't know what I thought—he was in a manic state, he'd installed decompression enhancements without telling me. Something to explain how he wasn't dead. Then I saw his face . . .

"His eyes—they were completely black. As if they'd been replaced. His mouth and nose were sealed over. I still tried to pull him back, but he was so strong, even stronger than my powered suit. He tossed me towards the *Queen.* I don't know what he was, but once he'd eaten the food the ship had made for him, he wasn't human anymore. Ayanti was gone."

"What did you do?" Saga knew the answer already, but she wanted to hear it from Wei herself.

"I didn't have a choice." Wei looked at Saga, eyes pleading. "I thought he was going to destroy our ship. I went back and took control of the anticollision systems and I . . . I burned him up. I burned him until he was nothing but a cinder. And then I put everything back in the *Queen,* and I mothballed it, and I ran away."

She closed her eyes again, took a shuddering breath. "I came back to the belt with nothing. I told his family that he'd died on a mission and I couldn't recover his body. I loved him. I really did. I *had* to do it. You need to understand."

~

Her story over, Wei huddled in the chair. If she was hoping for some sort of absolution, she wasn't going to get it. Saga couldn't imagine doing what the other woman had done, even in self-defense. And to do it to someone she loved—to Michel?

The nightmarish image of Gregor's disintegrating corpse surfaced in her mind, and Saga's anger bloomed, a red-hot coal in her chest.

She stood up. "What happened to Gregor was your fault. You knew what the ship's food would do to him and you didn't say anything."

Wei stared at the floor. "I told him to keep his suit on."

"But you didn't tell him *why*. You didn't tell any of us anything. *You* killed him, and you incinerated him. Just like Ayanti."

Wei didn't react. Saga wanted to kick her.

"Was there even a company who wanted this route?" Michel said.

"Yes." Wei looked up. "I didn't have the resources to come back on my own, but when I heard about their colonization plans I convinced them to fund this mission."

"But why?" Saga said. "Why did you bring *us* here? Revenge?"

"Not just that. I couldn't stop thinking about the *Queen,* lurking out here like a predator in the dark. I had to send it out of the solar system."

"Why didn't you do it the first time?" Michel said.

"Because she couldn't." Saga jabbed her finger at Wei. "Ayanti was the hacker. You didn't know how to override the navigation controls, how to make the ship's mind do what you wanted."

"I tried," Wei snapped. "But none of my hacks worked. I knew I would need experts." She paused. "And you wouldn't have come if I had told you the truth."

"We're calling for help now, Wei. I don't care what you think." Saga turned to Michel, who was already accessing the communications system.

He frowned. "That's . . . odd."

"What is?"

He swore, tapped at the control surfaces. "The comms system is working, but no signals are getting out. It's as if—"

Saga turned to Wei. "What have you done to the ship?"

"What I had to," she whispered. She picked up her helmet and put it back on.

Michel activated the ship's external cameras. He clicked around until he found what he was looking for: the antenna array was twisted and scorched, melted into an abstract sculpture. Wei had turned the anticollision lasers on it.

"That's it, then," he said. "We don't have the *Sigurd,* and now we don't have working antennae. We can't call for help." He loomed over Wei, furious. "Are you insane?"

Wei stood and he grabbed her shoulder. She hit him hard in the chest and he fell backward, her blow knocking him across the room in the bridge's low gravity.

Saga took a step forward, but stopped when she saw the gleam of metal. Wei had Gregor's cutting laser in her gloved hand. "Don't move. I don't want to hurt you if I don't have to." She pointed the laser at the console and fired, plastic and glass crackling and smoking as the beam ran over it. She swept it down across Michel's and Saga's pressure suits, then backed her way to the stairs and slid out of sight.

Saga ran to Michel's side. "Are you okay?"

He touched his chest gingerly. "I'll survive. But I think she broke a rib. Maybe a couple."

She helped him up. "Careful. I'll get the first-aid kit."

"Just be quick," he said. "Who knows what she's up to."

Saga helped Michel to a seat at the console, then grabbed the kit from their half-melted pile of gear. As she applied compression tape to his torso, his fingers tapped on the bridge's undamaged control surfaces, interrupted by sharp gasps of pain.

She looked at the display. "What are you doing?"

"If we don't have comms, we need helm control so we can fly to safety. I'm trying to see if I can transfer it from the console she wrecked."

"Trying?"

"Wei locked us out *and* she zapped the nav systems with that laser. I'm not sure I can do it." He swore. "Can you locate her? Use the internal cameras."

Saga started flicking through the video feeds, then realized there was a better way. "Ship," she said. "Could you show me the other person on board? The one not in this room."

The view changed in front of her. She saw the back of Wei's head for a moment. The image flickered, shifting to another camera. There was a cascade of sparks, a tiny sun in Wei's hand.

"She's welding something," Saga said. "Ship," she said. "Where is she?"

"The person you are observing is at the drive access hatch," the ship said. "She is inside the propulsion section."

"Michel, she's going to the drive. Can she manually control it from there?"

He frowned, searched the air for invisible information. "Yes," he said. "I think so. She doesn't need to do anything fancy, just turn it on and leave it on until we run out of propellant. Then we're completely screwed."

"So we have to stop her. You can't do anything from here?"

He shook his head. "I'm locked out. We have to get to her."

"Ship," Saga said. "Will you help us?"

"I am happy to assist," the ship said. "What help do you need?"

"We have to get to the propulsion section, but not through the drive access hatch."

"There is no other way to access the propulsion section from inside the *Martian Queen.*"

"Unfortunately Wei fucking welded the hatch shut—unless you have another cutting laser."

"I'm sorry, but you will have to talk to the head of engineering to obtain work tools. I cannot locate this crewmember."

Saga looked at Michel.

"I was already in engineering," he said. "When we looked around the ship. You know I like tools; I wanted to see what they had. It was stripped clean. Gregor must have brought the laser with him from the *Sigurd*."

Saga thought of something. "Ship, you said we couldn't access propulsion from inside the *Queen*. What about outside? Is there external access?"

"There is one emergency hatch," the ship replied. "As well as four maintenance ports for mech access."

Michel looked at their gear. "Is there any hope?"

Saga lifted the torso section of her suit. A scorched line cut through it. "They're both ruined. They'll never hold pressure."

Michel slammed his hand on the console. "There's got to be something else. This is a spaceship, for God's sake."

"Come on." Saga held out her hand. "There is something we can try."

They raced to Gregor's room, Michel grunting and holding his side. At the doorway, Saga felt something drop in the pit of her stomach.

Michel nudged her. "You're sure this was his?"

She nodded, looking at the space before her. It was

empty. No suit was crammed under the bed. "Ship, did you clean this room?"

The ship's voice came from a panel by the door. A light pulsed gently as the ship spoke. "The guest has left the ship, so housekeeping was activated."

"We need something he left behind."

There was silence. "Ship?"

The ship finally spoke. "The materials in the room are no longer retrievable."

"What does that mean?" Michel said.

"It doesn't sound good. Ship, are there any other pressure suits on board? Anywhere?"

"I'm sorry, but my stores inventory is incomplete," the ship said. "Ship systems have been in hibernation mode. I do not currently have a complete knowledge of all items on board."

"*Fokk,*" Saga said. She kicked the door frame and her foot went through the wall. "What the hell?" She bent and examined the hole her foot had made. The edges of the wall material crumbled in her hand. Wei had described the ship being hollowed out, and here was the proof. She felt a prickling across her skin.

"Michel," she said.

But her husband was occupied, tapping quick commands in the air, his gaze far away. "I've got an idea," he said. "Follow me."

~

The lifeboat section had three hatches.

"They have to have suits, right?" Michel said. He paused for a moment, thinking. "They'll also have emergency beacons. Food and environment systems to keep a hundred or more people alive for as long as rescue might take . . ."

Saga looked at him in surprise. "You think we should abandon ship?"

Michel nodded. "This isn't our ship. It isn't our fight. Wei can do whatever she wants after we've set off. We can switch on the beacons and wait to be rescued."

"Ship," Saga said. "Open the lifeboats. Prep for evacuation."

"Is this a drill?" the ship asked. "There has not been a declared emergency."

"It *is* an emergency," Saga said. "Abandon ship. Sound the alarms, do whatever you have to."

"I do not detect any emergency conditions. I cannot initiate an abandon ship without senior crew authorization or a confirmed emergency."

Saga looked at Michel, frustrated. He frowned, then his face brightened. "Actually, it *is* a drill," he said. "We need to test the lifeboat systems. Please grant us access."

There was silence from the ship. Saga was intensely

aware of Wei, working away in the drive section. They didn't have time. Then the hatches opened with a click and hum.

They stepped down and stopped in the first hatchway, startled by what they saw.

The inside of the lifeboat was in motion, a slow shifting like the surface of a deep river. What looked like mother-of-pearl coated the walls and floor. The layout was still vaguely recognizable as a spacecraft: consoles and chairs, the outlines of compartment doors. But everything shimmered with an otherworldly iridescence. A ripple moved through it, spreading from where they stood, as if their presence had disturbed something living.

"No," Michel said. *"No."*

"The next one." Saga grabbed his arm and they both backed out of the lifeboat. A few steps took them to the second open hatch. Inside everything looked reassuringly normal.

Michel opened a compartment, revealing rows of emergency supplies: water containers, packages of nutritional bars. Saga tapped a control on the console at the stern of the craft. Lights flickered to life.

"Okay," she said. "We're in business." She closed her eyes in relief. They'd just have to override the safeties that kept the lifeboat docked to the ship, and they could escape the doomed *Queen*.

"Um. Saga?"

She opened her eyes, looked at her husband. He held something in his hand.

"What's that?"

"A food bar," he said. "I thought we'd better test one."

He tossed it to her and she caught it. It was rubbery, lighter than it should have been. She put it on the floor and stepped on it, and the bar popped. A simulacrum. She turned and kicked the metal wall beside her and her foot went through it. The console lights went out.

Michel pulled items from the storage lockers. Empty water containers, more useless emergency rations. He kept going, tossing everything onto the floor.

"Stop it," Saga said. He ignored her. He tugged at the compartment door and the whole thing came away in his hands. He fell backward and hit the floor with a grunt, his face contorted in pain.

She crouched, her hand on his shoulder. "Just stop." She tossed aside the broken door. "You're making it worse. You need to lie down, you have to rest."

Michel sighed. "How much worse can it get?"

"There must be something we can do, but not if you puncture your lung or start an internal bleed."

She helped him hobble back through the hatch, then told the ship to open the nearest stateroom door. She laid him down on the bed and covered him with a blanket she found in the small closet. The bed felt solid enough. She took a couple of patches from the medical kit she'd retrieved from her suit and put them on his neck.

He touched them. "What's that?"

"For the pain." She stroked his forehead while the patches took effect. She'd added a sedative to the painkillers. She didn't need him running around, trying to fix the unfixable. Not now.

He closed his eyes. In a minute he was asleep.

Saga sat on the edge of the bed and tried not to give in to despair. She leaned her head against the wall and felt a rumbling vibration. She picked up her first-aid kit and dropped it, watching as it fell slowly to the floor. It landed a few centimeters away from the point she'd let it go. Wei had gained control of propulsion, and she was adjusting their course. They were under thrust again.

She could see it now. Wei would burn the engines until the ship was headed out of the solar system, as she'd always intended. Or maybe she'd steer it straight into Jupiter, just to be sure. Either way they would all die.

There was a knock on the door. Startled, Saga stood up and touched the peephole display. The female synth named Krasivaya stood outside, dressed in a cream-colored shift. She wore a jeweled headdress, and her lips were silver, her cheeks dusted with reddish powder.

Saga opened the door.

"Dinner is served," Krasivaya said. "Please join us in the dining room."

Saga closed the door, her heart thudding. She remembered an old movie about the *Titanic*, the musicians playing on deck while the ship sank. She imagined the synths and projections re-creating past feasts long after the three remaining humans had rotted away.

She sat back down on the bed and took inventory. She'd removed the thigh pouch from her suit when they left the bridge. As well as the first-aid kit, it held other things: a protein bar; a suit power cell. The black dress she'd worn that first night on the *Queen*.

Saga picked up the folded dress. The fabric had the weight and feel of silk. If the ship, or whatever had taken over the ship, had extruded this, it had done so with great skill. And it had crafted it for *her:* the dress fit perfectly.

Wei thought the *Queen* had some sort of contamination. She'd used her biocontainment gear and found nothing. But no contamination could create something like that dress. That showed *intent*. Whatever Michel would have called it, she was sure of it now: the ship was haunted. Some intelligence, some spirit, had taken possession. If it had been malevolent, it could have easily dealt with them. Even when it took control of Gregor's body, it had only been correcting the ship's course. Just as Wei's partner had returned stolen property, fixing the damage.

So if it wasn't malevolent, perhaps they had a chance. Perhaps there was still something she could do.

She sat watching Michel sleep. She had been slow to agree to marry him, then she'd resisted his talk of children. Everything had to be pushed off to some future where she could be *sure*. Sure that they both wouldn't somehow change.

Her parents started out happy, like everyone else. Then that happiness soured and twisted. She always feared that would happen to her and Michel someday.

"I wish . . . ," she said. "I wish . . ." She had wished for a lot of things that hadn't come true. When she had driven with her mother on their trip around the ring road, she'd wished that her father would leave them. That they'd come back to the house and all his things would be gone. It would just be the two of them, happy together.

But when they had arrived at the small house with the red roof, her father had been standing in the doorway. At the sight of him something in her, some ember of hope, had winked out.

What did she have left now?

Krasivaya was still outside, patiently waiting, a message from the *Queen*.

Saga began to get changed.

~

Wearing the black dress, Saga followed Krasivaya down the corridor. They stopped at the dining-room doors and Saga looked at the carving for a moment. One section showed a stag on a rocky outcropping. In the sky above gleamed a comet, its long tail silvery with the same opalescent shimmering as the lifeboat in flux.

Behind the doors came the sound of clinking forks and conversation. Krasivaya pushed and the doors opened. They were back at the dinner party.

As Saga walked over to the tables she searched for a familiar face, but the man in the turban was not among the diners. Their fashions were even older now. In the corner a string quartet played. She was witnessing one of the earliest voyages, perhaps the first.

Saga sat down in an empty chair. Across from her, the projection of a woman who'd been sipping from a wineglass vanished, replaced by the man she'd seen before, both here and in Wei's photograph.

"You're Ayanti, aren't you? Wei's partner."

The man looked at her. He didn't speak, but she thought she saw something in his eyes. Some subtle change.

"What do I do?" Saga said.

The man glanced to the back of the room and Saga

followed his gaze. A table had been set up near the bar. She recognized the male synth standing behind it, wearing his uniform. He was carving from a roast.

When she looked back Ayanti was gone. The wine-drinking woman had returned.

She stood and walked to the bar. The male synth nodded and held out a plate, which she took. On the table next to him were sauces and salvers, bowls of vegetables. He served her a generous slice from the roast, then put a little of everything else on her plate.

Saga returned to her seat. The beef on her plate looked real enough. Pink in the middle, a trace of juices around the edge. The vegetables had grill marks. But the only scent came from her own unwashed body.

She picked up her knife and fork, cut a small piece of beef, and lifted it to her lips. She hesitated, remembering Wei's description of Ayanti's black eyes, his sealed mouth and nose. But she'd come this far; there was no backing out.

The roast had a faint flavor, not unpleasant, but definitely not meat. She chewed and swallowed, feeling a prickling of sweat on her forehead. She forced herself to eat some vegetables. Everything was room temperature and had the same mild taste. Like milk, bread, or potato dumplings without seasoning, bland and comforting.

Then she sat and waited.

Around her the recorded conversation ebbed and flowed, teetering at the edge of her understanding. Words burbled up, but she couldn't make out complete sentences. Time passed. She couldn't have said how much. Her eyes were closed. She imagined that she was drifting in darkness, cold and alone. The immensity of space enveloped her.

"Darling." She opened her eyes. Krasivaya stood beside her, holding out her hand. "Come with me."

Saga took her hand. Her thoughts were muddled, as if she'd been woken from a long sleep. The synth's fingers were warm and dry. "What happens now?"

Krasivaya laughed. "Music and dancing, of course." She tugged and Saga stood.

"No," Saga said. "I have things to do." She wobbled, the room spinning. She felt hot, unwell. A sick realization that she'd made a terrible mistake washed over her.

She staggered to the door. It opened and she was out in the corridor.

∼

As she walked Saga rubbed an itch at her side, just over the hip bone. The dress felt slick under her fingers. Its fibers were artfully interlinked long-chain polymers: she saw their structure in her head. She knew how to tweak the ship printer to extrude them.

She walked, more steadily now. When she ran a hand against the wall, her fingers left shimmering trails. She came to the passageway to the propulsion module. The door's edges were scorched by Wei's welding. She wished she could just kick her way through, but she knew that the ship's long process of transformation had not yet hollowed out the stern.

She left the spin module and came to the cargo area, floating in front of the door to the compartment Wei had evacuated. After Gregor ruined the docking port she'd made it into a temporary air lock to help them escape.

Saga touched the door and closed her eyes. Her vision dimmed, then brightened again. If she focused she realized she could see Wei: she was attacking the reactor housing, laser in hand, still in her suit.

Wei was a parasite, an itching, burrowing thing that had to be removed.

Saga reached out and twisted some internal muscle, and the lights went off in the propulsion module.

"Nice try," Wei said. "Whoever figured that out. But you're too late." Wei flicked her suit lights on, illuminating the space. She'd already cut pieces of plating from the wall, exposing armored and shielded conduits. She adjusted her laser and started cutting again.

Saga felt a tingling in her hip where the laser touched metal. Her body was the ship. Her body was also a frail thing of flesh and bone, floating in the hallway by the cargo hatch. Like the metal body, the frail body was changing. She had to wait for it to finish.

She was the *third* body; something had gone wrong with the first two. Whatever had infected them had not understood how a human body worked. It had operated Ayanti and Gregor like a crude puppeteer. But it had learned.

"Oh." She made a sound: lungs forcing air past wobbling flesh to make noise signifying understanding.

Saga came and went. Sometimes she was herself. Sometimes she was the ship. Sometimes she was a child in a small room, curled under her bed while her parents raged in the house below. Wishing she could melt into the air itself and escape.

The lights went out and Saga was blind. Her new senses could no longer feel the propulsion module. Wei had succeeded in cutting it off from the rest of the ship. She had control now. The rest of the *Queen* switched to emergency power. Lights dimmed, doors closed. Essential systems only.

Saga's body had curled in on itself. She straightened out as she inhabited it fully once more, the rest of the ship receding, but not gone. It was in her consciousness, but manageable now. She felt her skin tighten. Her nose and throat closed, constricted by newly grown muscles. The changes had not quite finished, but she had run out of time. The door opened in front of her and she pulled herself through.

When it closed the air was removed from the room. Then the second door opened. She felt a million pin-pricks across her skin, a dangerous tension in her joints. Ahead of her she saw the rip in the ship's hull where the *Sigurd* had broken free. She floated to the hole and pushed herself through into the blackness of space.

The stars lit the sky.

A part of her was startled to the point of incomprehension. She should be dead. But here she was, grasping handholds and pulling herself across the hull of the *Queen,* heading aft toward the propulsion module. Holding her breath, somehow unaffected by the lack of atmosphere.

At the propulsion module she focused her attention on the emergency hatch. There were red arrows painted on it, and warnings in six languages. A red light glowed beside the manual hatch control. The hatch couldn't be opened from the outside while the inside was under pressure. There was no way she could trigger it without access to the module's control systems. And Wei had cut her off.

She was running out of air. She felt the ache building

in her chest. In her mind she could see the module's layout. The four maintenance ports. The largest one was by the starboard radiator grid. She pulled her way to it, moving from handhold to handhold.

She wrapped her legs around a radiator strut for leverage and removed the port cover. Then she opened the secondary pressure hatch. The port was barely fifteen centimeters in diameter.

Saga could fit an arm or a leg, but not herself. Not as this human body.

She pushed back and looked up the length of the *Queen*. Mars was a red dot; Earth was a bright point of light on the other side of the sky, the moon a faint glimmer next to it. An immensity of space and time surrounded the ship. The few days since they'd broken into the *Queen* were nothing compared to the years the liner had traveled between the two worlds. And those decades were nothing compared to . . . to what? She had a sense of darkness and a slow drift. Geologic time and distance. A span of years that made her life seem like the brief spark of an ember floating up from a fire.

She focused her attention, and schematics blossomed in her mind. A safety system: a series of explosive bolts around the propulsion module. They could be manually triggered with the correct codes, jettisoning the entire module in an emergency.

The reactor and engines, Wei—they would just float away. The *Queen* would continue on without them, diminished, cooling.

It was the only choice left. Everything that had happened to her before was so inconsequential. Her entire existence was nothing compared to the life that inhabited the *Queen*.

She started moving toward the explosive bolts.

As she moved she reached out, her hands grasping grip points and struts. Something shone on her left hand, reflecting the far-off sun—a metal circle. It had significance. It jarred something loose in her. She was not just a tool.

Was her life nothing? Maybe. But she remembered her mother, her grief. And she saw Michel, asleep in the stateroom. She knew this was an actual image, not just a memory. He was lying there right now. Still himself. Still worth saving.

He would die if she jettisoned the propulsion module.

She held on to the realization. There had to be another way. She reached out with her mind again and dove into the vast, dark sea of time and memory that lived in the ship.

She wandered for what could have been days, weeks. The *Martian Queen* was a million fireflies in the shape of a spacecraft. She roamed the places between them. It was a wilderness, but there were paths if you knew how to look. She sensed the strange intelligence that inhabited the *Queen*. It was unfocused and tentative, driven by instinct more than anything. But she could affect it: she pushed and it reacted. She was a part of it now, and as she understood this, she realized she could change herself as well.

But.

She would not be the same, never again the same if she were to do this.

She conjured up the inn from her trip on the ring road with her mother. Opened the door and entered the warmth and light of the place. She curled up on the rug with the old chocolate Lab she'd fallen in love with as a girl and stroked his fur.

Saga had thought that coming out to the belt had been a sacrifice: her work would pay for the cure for her mother's broken mind. It would be her penance. But of course it had been another kind of running away, just as she'd fled Iceland in her teens. In the belt she lived much as she had back on Earth, constantly moving from place to place, from exploration to exploration. Always looking for the next experience. And she'd dragged Michel along, who'd come out of love for her.

That had not been a *real* sacrifice. She had not borne the cost of it: everyone else in her life had.

She looked at Michel and made her decision.

~

Time passed, and Saga came back to herself, clinging to the side of the ship. The aching need to breathe was gone. Her limbs felt longer, looser. Her whole being was lighter. She knew what to do now. She slid forward, grasped the edge of the maintenance port's pressure hatch, and *poured* herself through. She traveled the darkness, down into the heart of the ship.

There was another hatch at the end of the port. It was trivial to open it now. She emerged into a dark chamber. She closed everything tightly as she moved through the spaces of the module, maintaining the ship's integrity. It was important, this part of the ship. Nothing had been changed here. Propulsion was sacred. Heat and light were food.

Saga came to the human space inside the module. She was still wearing the dress, still barefoot. There was frost in her hair; she shook her head and a drift of snow floated away, melting where it touched deck and walls.

Her connection to the rest of the ship was cut off by reactor shielding and by Wei's sabotage, but she was not alone. She had found a ghost among the fireflies and brought it with her. It followed her still as she floated through the narrow access corridor toward the reactor controls. She remembered Orpheus and Eurydice, the long ascent from the underworld, and his mistake.

Don't look back.

Wei was now working beneath the bulbous shape of the reactor housing. There was an acrid smell in the air. She'd been busy with her cutting laser, obviously trying to disable the reactor itself.

"Wei," Saga said. "Please stop."

Wei's body jerked with surprise. She let out a strangled noise as she quickly pulled herself out from under the housing and locked eyes with Saga.

Saga held out her hands, showing they were empty. Wei fumbled for the laser, pointed it at her. "Don't come any closer. I'll do it; you know I will."

"You don't know *what* you're doing," Saga said gently. "Do you? You don't understand what's happened to the ship. It isn't what you think."

Wei frowned at her. "How did you get in here? How did you get through the doors?"

Saga smiled. It was too difficult to explain. Wei's face narrowed with suspicion. "You're not really Saga, are you? You've been taken over." She lifted the laser, her trembling finger hovering over the activation stud.

"This isn't about me," Saga said. She felt unnaturally calm. The ghost was just around the corner now. "This is about something bigger than either of us. This ship has to remain safe. Michel has to remain safe."

There was a hum from the cutting laser, a flickering light, and a sharp burning smell. Saga looked down at the cut across her abdomen. She could feel that it had happened, but there was no pain. Perhaps this was shock. She frowned at Wei.

"It was an accident," Wei stammered. "I . . . I didn't mean to fire."

Saga looked down again. Her dress had melted, and under it the skin too. Her left hand had been in the path of the laser and two fingers tumbled through the air. She held her hand up, looking at the hollow space where her fingers had been.

She watched as the silvery stumps of her fingers slowly sealed themselves. She put her other hand on her abdomen, slipped a finger into the healing cut, felt the empty space behind it. "I'm a hollow person," she said, her voice full of wonder. "I don't *feel* hollow."

Wei lifted the laser, her face full of resolve. "I'm sorry," she said. Then her expression faltered. She looked over Saga's shoulder and Saga knew the ghost had arrived.

She turned. A familiar-looking long-limbed man, wearing a T-shirt and loose pants, floated beside her.

"Ayanti?" Wei said, her voice breaking. "Ayanti?"

Saga watched the man. He smiled, but didn't speak.

"I killed you," Wei said. "I burned you up." Tears glimmered in her eyes.

Ayanti continued to smile, his face serene.

Wei turned to Saga, anguish contorting her face. "Why won't he speak? What is this, some sort of trick?"

Saga shook her head. "I saw him in the dining room the first night we stayed here. I went looking and I found him. I didn't have time to retrieve everything, but he's still here. His memories remain in the ship."

"I'm sorry," Wei said to Ayanti's ghost. "I'm sorry I killed you."

"You didn't," Saga said. "You just destroyed his body. They didn't know how to integrate properly with a human, not then. But if you destroy the ship, Wei, he'll be gone forever."

Wei stared at her. "How do you know?"

"I gave up something of myself to make this body," Saga said. "I ate the food and became a part of this ship, and a part of whatever found it out here. I think it's something ancient. Something that just wants to live."

Ayanti reached out, held his hand open to Wei.

"He remembers," Saga said. "He remembers meeting you on Pallas. The fights and the making up. The adventures you had together. He remembers so much."

Wei shook her head. "No," she said. She pointed the laser at Ayanti. "You're not real. Neither of you are real."

Her hand trembled, and the laser cut Ayanti's head off. It tumbled, revealing its hollowness. The rest of him continued moving, pushing forward with outstretched hands. Wei frantically slashed at him with the laser. Flame flickered on his T-shirt. His leg was sliced open from thigh to kneecap.

All of Wei's attention was focused on Ayanti. The anguish in her face as she fired at him. Saga reached her in a single lunge and plucked the laser from her hands. Wei fought back, but Saga was stronger now. She threw the laser and it disappeared down the access corridor.

Wei struggled against her, screamed. Finally she broke down, tears clinging to her eyes. Saga held on to her until she stopped moving.

"Just kill me," Wei said. "Or are you going to force me to eat the food too? Is that it?"

"No," Saga said. "Worse than that. I'm going to save you."

~

The third lifeboat had only been partially digested. After Saga brought Wei back, she opened the hatch and performed a quick analysis. The radio still worked, and there was enough edible food and water for a hundred souls. Life support would be operational once the changes were reversed. She set the process in motion. Matter was shuffled, reorganized to regrow wires and circuits, the delicate meshwork of filtration systems and atmosphere scrubbers.

Under her command, the male synth reattached the power and data cabling to the propulsion module and welded the reactor plating back on. Krasivaya collected the pieces of Ayanti and brought them to her. Saga didn't allow Michel to witness the reassembly: he would have a difficult enough time grasping how Ayanti came into being.

It was still hard to believe she had made another person from her own body. She thought of her frozen embryos, waiting on Ceres.

In the stateroom, Saga gave Michel an edited version of events, but he didn't understand. "You said the lifeboat would be back the way it was," Michel said.

"Better," she said. "I fixed a few flaws along the way."

He looked at her. "So fix yourself too. Make yourself the way you were before."

Saga took his hand. It was warm, alive. "It's not that simple."

"Of course it is." He pulled her closer. Held her tight. "You're my wife, and you're coming back with me."

She felt an ache inside that she knew would never completely die away. A part of her would remain human, whatever happened. "I've gone too far, Michel; I've changed too much. But even if I could go back with you, the *Queen* would still be out here."

She paused, trying to put into words what she knew to be true.

"Imagine seeds. Imagine them floating for millions of years, waiting to come into contact with a machine of some sort. Maybe they evolved in some civilization on the other side of the galaxy. They're like viruses; they find machines and they use them to reproduce. They've been harvesting the *Queen* for years. Getting ready."

She could feel the next generation of seeds sleeping, distributed throughout the ship's hollow skin. There were so many of them. She couldn't help but feel a maternal warmth at the thought.

"If we all left in that lifeboat," she continued, "what do you think would happen? The ship would change course again, back to its original orbit around the sun. One day it would come apart like a dandelion clock in the wind. Most of the seeds would never find anything. Jupiter would suck them up, or they'd drift off into interstellar space. But some would reach Earth, Mars, ships, and habitats. They would grow." She left the implications unsaid.

Michel let go of her. "Then you should have let Wei destroy the ship," he said bitterly. He would not meet her eyes.

"You would have died," she said quietly. "And it would have sent out seeds before it died, too. Anyway, who are we to say it should be destroyed? If I stay I can guide the *Queen* safely out of the solar system. This is the only way."

"I can't believe you're sending me off in a lifeboat with this woman who caused everything. I don't get a choice at all?"

"No," Saga said. "Not this time. Go back to Earth and see my family. Tell them I'm sorry. Tell them it's important, what I'm doing."

Michel shook his head. He got up from the bed and went to the small desk in the corner. He sat at the desk, his back to her.

Saga went to the door. There was a limit to what could be said with words.

Wei was in the room across the corridor. Saga closed her eyes so she could see inside. Ayanti sat with her on the bed. The ship had upgraded the crude body she had fashioned. It now held his memories, his thoughts. He could talk. They'd been talking for a long time now, holding hands. She could see the tear tracks on Wei's cheeks.

Saga walked the corridors again, past the model ships and the hollow carvings on the doors. The dining room that still echoed with the sounds of past dinner parties as the ship brought them to life, spurred by the mimetic instincts of the organisms that inhabited the *Queen*.

She'd seen this ship as a sterile, forgotten thing. She remembered her disappointment when she realized that it would have made a terrible interactive. That whatever stories she would have told here would have been clichéd and uninspired.

Now there was something else. There had been deaths here, but also life. She began to think about a new interactive. A way to pay tribute to Gregor and Ayanti, and to her mother. Something that captured the feeling of being part of a machine that was being remade. That might just become something greater than the sum of its parts. She had lots of time to work on it. It would be the last and the most important thing she would ever create.

~

She found Michel on the bridge, curled on the floor, surrounded by crumbs from the steak sandwich they'd left there. She stood and watched him, feeling a wave of tenderness for what he'd tried to do. Then she reached out and undid the changes that had begun within him, disconnecting him from the ship, returning his cells to their former selves.

She carried him back to the stateroom. Across the hall, Wei slept peacefully in Ayanti's arms. He had already placed a sedative patch on her neck, and Saga did the same to Michel.

When the time came, Saga stood at the lifeboat hatch as Ayanti and Krasivaya gently carried their sleeping cargo to the lifeboat and deposited them inside.

They came back out and stood with her and the male synth as the hatch closed. In her mind's eye, she saw the puffs of gas as the lifeboat was pushed away from the *Queen*. Then the boat's small engine fired and it quickly dwindled, heading for an orbit that would make their rescue possible, though it would take months. Perhaps Michel and Wei would come to some sort of accommodation in that time. Perhaps not.

She felt a rumble as the *Queen's* own engines came to life. A part of her mind carefully worked to persuade the ship that it was okay to leave this small yellow sun behind. There were other places.

Saga could still cry, so she did that for a while. Then she turned to Ayanti and the two synths.

"Come," she said. "We have work to do."

About the Authors

ANDREW NEIL GRAY and **J. S. HERBISON** are partners in life as well as in writing. *The Ghost Line* is their first fiction collaboration but won't be their last: a novel is also in the works. They have also collaborated in the creation of two humans and preside over a small empire of chickens, raspberries, and dandelions on Canada's west coast. You can find Andrew Neil Gray at http://andrewneilgray.com and @andrewneilgray on Twitter. You can find J. S. Herbison at http://jsherbison.com.

TOR · COM

Science fiction. Fantasy. The universe.

And related subjects.

*

More than just a publisher's website, *Tor.com*
is a venue for **original fiction, comics,** and
discussion of the entire field of SF and fantasy,
in all media and from all sources. Visit our site
today—and join the conversation yourself.